"You're very good at what you do. I certainly won't deny that."

"What I do?" Dalton asked.

"The whole seduction bit. The oh-so-casual touches, those sexy, intimate smiles. Stepping closer and closer until I can't focus on anything but you. I imagine most women probably melt in a big puddle at your feet."

The cynicism in her voice smarted. "But not you?"

"I'm sorry if that stings your pride but I'm just not interested," Jenny answered. "I believe I told you that."

"So you did," Dalton agreed. "But are you so sure about that, Ms. Boyer?"

Against the howl of all his instincts, he stepped closer again. The hunger inside him threatened whatever remained of his self-control and his sanity.

"Ye-es," Jenny said, though that single word came out breathy, hushed.

"I think we know that's not precisely true," he murmured, then leaned down slowly....

DALTON'S UNDOING

RAEANNE THAYNE

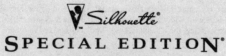

SPECIAL EDITION

Published by Silhouette Books

America's Publisher of Contemporary Romance

 **SILHOUETTE BOOKS**

ISBN 0-373-24764-8

DALTON'S UNDOING

Books by RaeAnne Thayne

Silhouette Special Edition

Light the Stars #1748
Dancing in the Moonlight #1755
Dalton's Undoing #1764

Silhouette Intimate Moments

The Wrangler and the Runaway Mom #960
Saving Grace #995
Renegade Father #1062
*The Valentine Two-Step #1133
*Taming Jesse James #1139
*Cassidy Harte and the Comeback Kid #1144
The Quiet Storm #1218
Freefall #1239
Nowhere To Hide #1264
†Nothing To Lose #1321
†Never Too Late #1364
The Interpreter #1380

*Outlaw Hartes
†The Searchers

RAEANNE THAYNE

lives in a graceful old Victorian nestled in the rugged mountains of northern Utah, along with her husband and two young children. Her books have won numerous honors, including several readers' choice awards and a RITA® Award nomination by the Romance Writers of America. RaeAnne loves to hear from readers. She can be reached through her Web site at www.raeannethayne.com or at P.O. Box 6682, North Logan, UT 84341.

To Jared, for twenty wonderful years
filled with joy and laughter
and midnight trips to the store when I run out
of printer ink. I love you dearly!

Chapter One

Some little punk was stealing his car.

Seth Dalton stood on the sidewalk in front of his mother's house, the puppy leashes in his hand forgotten, and watched three years of sweat, passion and hard work take off down the road with a flash of tail lights and the squeal of rubber.

Son of a bitch.

He stood looking after it for maybe fifteen seconds, trying to comprehend how anybody in Podunk Pine Gulch would have the stones to steal his 1969 Matador red GTO convertible.

Who in town could possibly be stupid enough to dream he could get more than a block or two without somebody sitting up and taking notice that Seth wasn't the one behind the wheel and raising the alarm?

Just how far did the bastard think he would get? Not very, if Seth had anything to say about it. He'd worked too hard on his baby to let some sleazebag drive her away.

"Come on, kids. Fun's over." He jerked the leashes, grateful the dogs weren't in midpee, and dragged the two brindle Australian herder pups up the sidewalk and back into the house.

Inside, the members of his family were crowded around his mother's dining-room table playing one of their cutthroat games of Risk.

Looked like Jake and Maggie were kicking butt. No surprise there, with his middle brother's conniving brain and his wife's military experience. The Dalton clan was in its usual teams, Jake and Maggie against his mother and stepfather, with his oldest brother, Wade, and wife, Caroline, making up the third team.

That was the very reason he'd volunteered to take the puppies out for their business in the first place. It was a little lonely being the solitary player on his side of the table. Usually he teamed up with Natalie—but it was a little disheartening to find his nine-year-old niece made a more cutthroat general than he. She was in the family room watching a video with her brothers, anyway.

The only one who looked up from strategizing was his mother.

"Back so soon? That was fast!" Marjorie crooned the words, not to him but to the puppies—or her half of the dynamic duo anyway. She picked up the birthday gift he'd given her and nuzzled the little male pup.

"You're so good. Aren't you so good? Yes, you are. Come give Mommy a birthday kiss."

"Don't have time, sorry," Seth said drily.

He ignored the face she made at him and reached for the keys to Wade's pickup from the breakfast bar.

"I'm taking your truck," he called on his way out the door.

Wade looked up, a frown of concentration on his tough features. "You're what?"

He paused at the door. "Don't have time to explain, but I need your truck. I'll be back. Mom, keep an eye on Lucy for me."

"I just washed that truck," his brother growled. "Don't bring it back all muddy and skanky."

He wasn't even going to dignify that with a response, he decided, as he headed down the stairs. He didn't have the time, even if he could have come up with a sharp response.

Wade's truck rumbled to life, smooth and well-tuned like everything in Seth's oldest brother's life. He threw it in gear and roared off in the direction the punk had taken his car.

If he were stealing a car, which road would he take? Pine Gulch didn't offer a lot of escape routes. Turning south would lead him through the houses and small business district of Pine Gulch. To the east was the rugged western slope of the Teton Mountains, which left him north and west.

He took a chance and opted to head north, where the quiet road stretched past ranches and farms with little traffic to notice someone in a red muscle car.

He ought to just call the police and report the theft. Chasing after a car thief on his own like this was probably crazy, but he wasn't in the mood to be sensible, not with thirty thousand dollars' worth of sheer horsepower disappearing before his eyes.

He pushed Wade's truck to sixty-five, keeping his eye out in the gathering twilight for any sign of another vehicle.

His efforts were rewarded just a moment later when

he followed the curve of the road past Sam Purdy's pond and saw a flash of red up ahead.

His brother's one-ton pickup rumbled as he poured on the juice and accelerated to catch the little bugger.

With its 400-cubic-inch V8 and the three hundred and fifty horses straining under the hood, the GTO could go a hundred and thirty without breaking a sweat. Oddly enough, whoever had boosted it wasn't pushing her harder than maybe forty.

His baby puttered along fifteen miles below the speed limit and Seth had no problem catching up with her, wondering as he did if there was some kind of roving gang of senior-citizen car thieves on the loose he hadn't heard about.

He kept a respectable two-car length between them as the road twisted again. He knew this road and knew that just ahead was a straightaway that ran a couple of miles past farmland with no houses.

He couldn't see any oncoming traffic so he pulled into the other lane as if to pass and drew up alongside his baby, intent on getting a look at the thief.

He *was* a punk, nothing more. The kid behind the wheel was skinny, dark-haired, maybe fifteen, sixteen. He looked over at the big rumbling pickup beside him and he looked scared to death, eyes huge and wild in a narrow face.

Good. He should be, the little dickhead. Seth rolled the window down, wishing he could reach across, pluck the kid out of the car and wring his scrawny little neck.

"Pull over," he shouted through the window, even though he knew the kid wouldn't be able to hear him.

He must have looked like the Grim Reaper, Freddy Kruger and the guy from *The Texas Chainsaw Massacre* all rolled up into one, he realized later, and he should have predicted what happened next. If he'd been thinking straight, he would have handled the whole thing differently and saved himself a hell of a lot of trouble.

Even if the car thief couldn't hear Seth's words, obviously the message got through loud and clear. The kid sent him another wild, scared look and yanked the wheel to the right.

Seth growled out a raw epithet at the hideous sound of metal grinding against metal as the GTO scraped a mile marker post on the right. In reaction, the kid panicked and swerved too hard to the left and Seth groaned as his baby nosedived across the road and landed in an irrigation ditch.

At least it was blessedly empty this time of year.

The sun was just a sliver above the horizon and the November air was cold as Seth hurriedly parked the pickup and rushed to his car to make sure the kid was okay.

He jerked open the door and was petty enough for just a moment to enjoy the way the kid cringed against the seat like he thought Seth was ready to break his neck with his bare hands.

He felt like it, he had to admit. He had no doubt the GTO's paint was scraped all to hell from the run-in with the mile marker post and the left fender looked to be crumpled where she'd hit a concrete gate structure in the ditch.

He held on to his anger while he checked the thief for any sign of injury.

"You okay?" he asked.

"Yeah. I…think so." The boy's voice shook a little but he warily took Seth's hand and climbed out of the car.

Seth revised downward his estimate of the boy's age, figuring him to be no older than thirteen or fourteen. Just old enough to start shaving more than once a month, by the look of it.

He had choppy dark hair worn longer than Hank Dalton would ever have let *his* sons get away with and he was dressed in jeans and a gray hooded sweatshirt about four sizes too big with some logo of a wild-looking music group Seth didn't recognize.

The kid seemed familiar but Seth couldn't immediately place him—odd, since he knew just about every kid in the small community. Maybe he was the son of one of the dozen or so Hollywood types buying up good grazing land for their faux ranches. They tended to stay away from the general population, maybe afraid the down-home friend-liness and family-centered values would rub off.

"My mom is gonna kill me," the kid moaned, burying his head in his hands.

"She can stand in line," Seth growled. "You have any idea how much work I've put into this car?"

The kid dropped his hands. Though he still looked terrified, he managed to cover it with a thin veneer of bravado. "You'll be sorry if you mess with me. My grandpa's a lawyer and he'll fry your ass if you try to lay a single hand on me."

Seth couldn't help a short, appreciative laugh even as the pieces clicked into place and he registered who the kid must be and why he had looked familiar.

With a grandfather who was a lawyer, he had to be the son of the new elementary school principal. Boylan. Boyer. Something like that.

He didn't exactly hang around with the elementary-school crowd but Natalie had pointed out her new prin-cipal and the woman's two kids one night shortly after school started when he'd taken his niece and nephews out to Stoney's, the pizza place in town.

His grandfather would be Jason Chambers, an attorney who had retired to Pine Gulch for the fishing five or six years back. His daughter had moved out to join him with her kids—no husband that Seth had heard about—when the principal position opened up at the elementary school.

"That lawyer in the family will probably come in handy, kid," he said now.

The punk groaned and his head sagged into his hands once more. "I am so dead."

He wasn't quite sure why but Seth was surprised to feel a few little pangs of sympathy for the kid. He re-membered all too well the purgatory of this age. Hormones firing, emotions jerking around wildly. Too much juice and nothing to do with it.

"Am I going to jail?"

"You boosted a car. That's a pretty serious crime. And you're a lousy driver, which is worse, in my book."

"I wasn't going to take her far. You've got to believe me. Just to the reservoir and back, I swear. That's all. When I saw the keys inside, I couldn't resist."

Damn. Had he really left the keys in the ignition? He looked inside and, sure enough, there they were, dangling from the steering column.

How had that happened? He remembered pulling up to his mother's house for her birthday dinner, then rushing out to take care of business when Lucy started to squat on the floor mats. Maybe in all the confusion, he had been in such a hurry to find a patch of grass before his puppy busted her bladder that he'd forgotten his keys.

What kind of idiot left his keys in a ride like this, just begging for the first testosterone-crazed teenager to lift her?

Him. He mentally groaned, grateful at least that the boy hadn't been hurt by their combined stupidity.

"What's your name, kid?"

The boy clamped his teeth together and Seth sighed. "You might as well tell me. I know your last name is Boyer and Jason Chambers is your grandpa. I'll figure out the rest."

"Cole," he muttered after a long pause.

"Come on, Cole. I'll give you a lift to your grandpa's house, then I'll come back and pull her out with one of my brothers."

"I can walk." He hunched his shoulders and shoved his hands in the pocket of his hooded sweatshirt.

"You think I'm going to leave you and your sticky fingers running free out here? What if you happen to find another idiot who's left his keys in his ride? Get in."

Though Cole still looked belligerent, he climbed into the passenger side of the pickup.

Seth had just started to walk around the truck to get in the driver's side when he saw flashing lights behind him.

Instead of driving past, the sheriff's deputy slowed and pulled up behind the GTO. Seth glanced at the boy and saw he'd turned deathly white and his breathing was coming fast enough Seth worried about him hyperventilating.

"Relax, kid," he muttered.

"I am relaxed." He lifted his chin and tried for a cool look that came out looking more like a constipated rabbit.

Seth sighed and closed his door again as he watched the deputy climb out of the vehicle. Before he even saw her face, he knew by the curvy shape that the officer had to be Polly Jardine, the only female deputy in the small sheriff's department.

She dimpled at him, looking not much different than she had in high school—cute and perky and worlds away from his idea of an officer of the law. Though she still looked like she should be shaking her pom-poms at a Friday night football game, he knew she was a tough and dedicated cop.

He imagined she inspired more than a few naughty fantasies around town involving those handcuffs dangling from her belt. But since her husband was linebacker-huge and also on the sheriff's department—and they were crazy about each other—those fantasies would only ever be that.

"Hey Seth. I thought that was your car. Man! What happened? You take the turn a little too fast?"

His gaze shifted quickly to the boy inside the truck then quickly back to Polly, hoping she hadn't noticed. He found himself strangely reluctant to throw Cole Boyer into the system.

"Something like that," he murmured.

She followed his gaze to the boy and speculation suddenly narrowed her eyes. "You sure that's the whole story?"

He leaned a hip against the truck, tilted his head and gave her a slow smile. "Would I lie to an officer of the law, darlin'?"

"Six ways from Sunday, *darlin'*." Though her words were tart, she smiled in a way that told him she remembered with fondness the few times they'd fooled around under the bleachers before Mitch Jardine moved into town and she had eyes for no one else. "But it's your car. If that's the way you want to play this, I won't argue with you."

"Thanks, Pol. I owe you."

"That's the new principal's kid, isn't it?"

He nodded.

"We've had a few run-ins with him in the few months they've been in town," she said. "Nothing big, breaking curfew, that kind of thing. You sure letting him off is the right thing to do for him? Today a joyride, tomorrow a bank robbery."

He didn't know anything except he couldn't bring himself to turn him in.

"For now."

"Let me know if you change your mind. I'm supposed to file an accident report but I'll just pretend I didn't see anything."

He nodded and waved goodbye then climbed into the truck. Cole Boyer watched him, his green eyes wary. "Am I going to jail?"

"No. Not today, anyway."

"Friggin' A!"

"Don't be so quick with the celebration there," he warned. "A week or two in juvie is probably going to look pretty damn good by the time your mother and grandfather get through with you. And that doesn't even take into account what you'll have to do to even the score with me."

She was late. As usual.

In one motion, Jenny Boyer shoved on slingbacks and shrugged into her favorite brocade jacket.

"Listen to Grandpa while I'm gone, okay?" she said, head tilted while she thrust a pair of conservative gold hoops into her ears.

"I always do." Morgan, her nine-year-old, going on fifty, sniffed just like a society matron finding something undesirable in her tea. "Cole is the one who doesn't like authority figures."

Didn't she just know it? Jenny sighed. "Well, make sure he listens to Grandpa, too."

Morgan folded her arms and raised an eyebrow. "I'll try, but I don't think he'll pay attention to either me or Grandpa."

Probably not, she conceded. Nobody seemed to be

able to get through to Cole. She'd thought moving to Idaho to live with her father would help stabilize her son, at least get him away from the undesirable elements in Seattle who were leading him into all kinds of trouble.

She had hoped his grandfather would give the boy the male role model he had lost with his own father's desertion. So much for that. Though Jason tried, Cole was so angry and bitter at the world—more furious with her now for uprooting him from his friends and moving him to this backwater than he was with his father for moving to another continent.

She glanced at her watch and groaned. The school board meeting started in ten minutes and she was scheduled to give a PowerPoint presentation outlining her efforts to raise the elementary school's performance on standardized testing. This was her first big meeting with the school board and she couldn't afford to blow it.

The therapist she'd gone to after the divorce suggested Jenny's chronic tardiness indicated some form of passive aggression, her way of governing a life that often felt beyond her control.

Jenny just figured she was too busy chasing after her hundreds of constantly spinning plates.

"I've got to run, baby. I'll be home before you go to sleep, I promise." She kissed her on the forehead, wondering as she headed out of her room if she had time to hurry down to the basement to say goodbye to Cole. No, she decided. Besides her time crunch, any conversation between them these days ended in a fight and she wasn't sure she was up for another one tonight.

"Bye, Dad," she called down the hall as she grabbed her laptop case and her purse. "Thanks for watching them!"

"Don't worry about a thing." Jason Chambers appeared in the doorway, wearing his favorite Ducks Un-limited sweater and jeans that made him look far younger than his sixty-five years. "Give 'em hell."

She mustered a distracted smile, grateful all over again that they'd been able to move past their compli-cated, stiff relationship of the past and find some measure of peace when she moved to Pine Gulch.

Juggling her bags and her keys, she yanked open the door and rushed out, then gave a shriek when she collided with a solid, warm male.

With a little gasp, Jenny righted herself, registering the muscles in that hard frame that seemed as immov-able as the Tetons. "I'm sorry! I didn't see you."

She knew who he was, of course. What woman in Pine Gulch didn't? With that slow, sexy smile and those brilliant blue eyes that seemed to see right into a woman's psyche to all her deepest desires, Seth Dalton was a difficult man to overlook.

Not that she didn't try her best. The youngest Dalton was exactly the kind of man she tried to avoid at all cost. She'd had more than enough, thank you very much, of smooth charmers who swept a woman off her feet with flowers and champagne only to leave her dangling there, hanging by her fingernails when they decide young French pastries are more to their taste.

What earthly reason would Dalton have for showing up at her doorstep? He had no children at her school, he was years past his own education and somehow she couldn't picture him as the type to bake cookies for the PTA fundraiser.

She couldn't think of anything else that would bring him to her door and the clock was ticking.

"May I help you, Mr. Dalton?"

Surprise flickered in those eyes for just a moment,

as if he hadn't expected her to know his name. "Just making a delivery."

She frowned, impatient and confused, as he reached around the door out of her view, tugging something forward. No something, someone—someone with a sullen scowl, a baggy sweatshirt and a chip the size of Idaho on his narrow shoulders.

"Cole!"

Beneath her son's customary sulky defiance, she thought she saw something else beneath the attitude, something nervous and on edge.

"What's going on? You're supposed to be down in your room working on geometry!" she exclaimed.

"Geometry blows. I went out."

"You went out," she repeated, frustration and bewilderment and a terrible sense of failure rising in her chest. How could she possibly reach the students at her school when she couldn't manage to find even the tiniest connection to her own son? "Out where? I didn't hear you leave."

"Ever hear of a window?" he sneered. Nothing new there. He had been derisive and mean to her before they ever came to Pine Gulch. He blamed her for everything wrong in his life, from his short stature to Richard's affair and subsequent abandonment.

She was mortified that a stranger had to witness it. She was even more mortified when Seth Dalton raised one of those sexy dark eyebrows and placed a firm hand on Cole's shoulder. "Now, do you really think that's the proper way to address your mother?"

Jenny gave the man a polite smile, wishing him to Hades. "Thank you, Mr. Dalton, for bringing him home, but I believe I can handle things from here."

For some reason, either her words or her tone seemed

to amuse him. His mouth quirked up and a masculine dimple appeared in his cheek briefly. "Can you, now? I'm afraid we still have a few matters of business to discuss. May I come in?"

"This isn't a good time. I'm late for a meeting."

"Sorry about that," he drawled, "but I'm afraid you'll have to make time for this."

He didn't wait for permission, just walked through her father's entry into the living room. She had no choice but to follow, noting as she went that Jason and Morgan were nowhere to be seen.

"Cole, you want to tell her what you've been up to?"

Her son crossed his arms, his expression even more belligerent, but again she caught a faint whiff of fear beneath it. Her stomach suddenly twisted with foreboding.

"What's going on? Cole, what is this about?"

He clamped his mouth shut, freezing her out again, but once more Seth Dalton placed a firm hand on his shoulder.

Cole suddenly seemed to find the carpet endlessly fascinating.

"Istolehisride," he mumbled in one breath and Jenny's heart stopped, hoping she'd heard wrong.

"You *what?*"

Cole finally lifted his gaze to hers. "I took his car, okay? What did he expect? He left the frigging keys in it. I was only going to take it for a mile or two. I figured I'd have it back before he even knew it was gone. But then I crashed…"

"You *what!* Are you hurt? Did you hurt anyone else?"

Cole shook his head. At least he had enough guilty conscience to look slightly ashamed.

"He scraped a mile marker post and front-ended into an irrigation ditch. The only thing damaged was my car."

She sagged into the nearest chair as her career

suddenly flashed in front of her eyes. She could almost hear the echo of gossip across shopping carts at DeLoy's, under the hair dryers at the Hairport and over beer at the Bandito.

Did you hear about that new principal's wild boy? She can't control him a lick. That little delinquent stole a car. Crashed it right into a ditch! Seems to me a woman who can't control her own son sure don't belong in that nice office down at the elementary school.

She screwed her eyes shut, wishing this was all some terrible dream, but when she opened them, Seth Dalton was still standing in front of her, as dangerous and sexy as ever.

"I am so sorry, Mr. Dalton. I...don't know what to say. Are you pressing charges?"

She thought she heard Cole make a small sound, but when she glanced at him, he looked as prickly and angry as ever.

"It's going to take me considerable work to fix it."

"We will, of course, cover any damages."

He suddenly sat down on the sofa across from her, crossing his boots at the ankle. "I had something else in mind."

She stiffened. "I'm an elementary school principal, Mr. Dalton. If you're looking for some kind of huge financial settlement, I'm afraid you're off the mark."

"I'm not looking for money." He glanced at Seth. "But I will need another set of hands while I'm doing the repair work. I figured the kid could work off the damages by helping me out with the repair work and around my ranch with my horses until the bodywork is done."

Cole straightened. "I'm no stupid-ass cowboy."

Seth Dalton gave him a measuring look. "No, from here you look like a stupid-ass punk who thinks he's living out some kind of video game. This isn't Grand Theft Auto, kid, where you can always hit the restart button. You broke it, now you're going to help me fix it. Unless you'd rather serve the time, of course."

Cole subsided back into his customary slouch as Jenny considered his proposal. Her gut wanted her to tell him to forget it. She didn't want her son to have anything to do with Pine Gulch's busiest bachelor.

Cole had had enough lousy male role models in his life—he didn't need a player like Seth teaching him all the wrong things about how to treat a woman.

On the other hand, her son stole the man's car—not only stole it, but wrecked the blasted thing. That he wasn't in police custody right now seemed nothing short of a miracle.

What choice did she have, really? Seth could easily have called the police. Perhaps he should have. Maybe a hard gut check with reality might be just what Cole needed to wake him up, as much as she hated the idea of her son in juvenile detention.

Seth Dalton was being surprisingly decent about this. From what little she knew about him—and she had to admit, most of her biased information came from over-heard conversations and breathless comments in the teacher's lounge about his many flirtations—she would have expected him to be hot-tempered and petulant.

Instead, she found him rational, calm, accommodating.

And extremely attractive.

She let out a slow, nervous breath. Was that the reason for her instinctive opposition to the man's rea-sonable proposal? Because he was sinfully gorgeous, with that thick, dark hair, eyes a stunning, heartbreak-ing blue and chiseled, tanned features that made him look as though he should be starring in Western movies?

He made her edgy and ill at ease and that alone gave her enough reason to wish for a way to avoid any further acquaintance between them. She was here in Pine Gulch to help her little family find some peace and healing—not to engage in useless, potentially harmful fantasies about a charming, feckless cowboy with impossibly blue eyes and a smile that oozed sex.

"I'll know better after I tow the car out to the ranch and take a look at her but from my initial look, I'd estimate there was about fix or six hundred dollars' damage," he was saying. "The way I figure it, if he worked for me a couple afternoons a week after school and Saturday mornings, we should be clear in a few months. Is that okay with you?"

She looked at Dalton and then at Cole, his arms still crossed belligerently across his chest, as if everyone else in the room was responsible for his troubles but himself.

He disdained everything about Idaho and would probably consider being forced to work on a ranch every bit as much punishment as going to juvenile detention, she thought.

"Yes. That's more than fair. Wouldn't you agree, Cole?"

Her son glared at both of them—and while Jenny felt her own temper kindle in automatic response, Seth met his look with cool challenge and Cole quickly dropped his gaze.

"Whatever," he muttered.

"Thank you," Jenny said again, walking with him to the door. "As tomorrow is Saturday, I'll drive him out to the Cold Creek in the morning. What time?"

"How does eight work for you?"

"We'll be there. I'm very sorry again about this. I can't imagine what he was thinking."

His smile was slow and wide and made her insides feel as if she'd just done somersaults down a steep, grassy hill.

"He's a teenage boy, so I'd guess he probably wasn't thinking at all. See you in the morning."

Jenny nodded, wondering why that prospect filled her with an odd mix of trepidation and anticipation.

Chapter Two

"This is totally lame," her son muttered the next morning. "Why do I have to give up a whole Saturday?"

Jenny sighed and cast Cole an admonishing glance across the width of her little Toyota SUV. "You prefer the alternative? I can call Mr. Dalton right now and tell him to go ahead and file charges if that's what you'd rather see happen here."

Cole sliced her a glare that told her quite plainly he considered *her* totally lame, too, but he said nothing.

"I don't think it's fair, either," Morgan piped up from the backseat. "Why does Cole always get to do the fun stuff? I want to help with the horses, too. Natalie says the Cold Creek horses are the prettiest, smartest horses anywhere. They've won all kinds of rodeo awards and they sell for *tons* of money. She said her uncle Seth knows more about horses than anybody else in the whole wide *world*."

"Wow. The whole wide world?" Sarcasm dripped from Cole's voice.

Morgan either didn't pick up on it or decided to ignore it. Judging from past experience, Jenny was willing to bet on the latter. Her daughter tended to ignore anything that didn't fit into her vision of the way the world ought to operate.

Even during her frequent hospital stays after bad asthma attacks, she always managed to focus on some silver lining, like a new friend or a particularly kind nurse.

"Yep," she said eagerly now, with as much pride in Seth Dalton as she might have had if he were *her* uncle instead of her best friend's. "People bring their horses to the Cold Creek from all over the place for him to train because he's so good."

"If he knows more than anyone else in the world, why is he stuck here in Buttlick, Idaho?"

Morgan's enthusiasm faded into a frown. "Just because you don't like it here, you don't have to call it mean words."

"I thought that was the name," Cole said with a sneer. "Right next to Hairy Armpitville and across the holler from Cow's Rectum."

"That's enough." Jenny's hands tightened on the steering wheel and she felt familiar stress weigh like a half-ton hay bale on her shoulders. She wasn't at all sure she was going to survive her son's adolescence.

"I hope you treat Mr. Dalton with more respect than you show me or your sister."

"How can I not, since apparently the man knows more about horses than anybody in the whole wide world?" Cole muttered.

Who was this angry stranger in her son's body? she wondered. Whatever happened to her sweet little man who used to love cuddling up with her at bedtime for stories and hugs? Who used to let her blow raspberries on his neck and would run to her classroom after school bubbling over with news of his day?

That sweet boy had been slipping away from her since the year he turned eleven, when Richard had moved out. Through the three ugly years since, he'd pulled deeper and deeper into himself, until now he only emerged on rare occasions.

This obviously wasn't going to be one of them.

Somehow Cole had come to blame her for the separation and divorce. She wasn't sure how or why she had come to bear that burden but the unfairness of it made her want to scream.

She, at least, had been faithful to her marriage vows. Though she hadn't been perfect by any means and had long ago accepted her share of responsibility for the breakup of her marriage, in her heart she knew she had tried to be a good wife.

She had supported Richard through his last years of medical school, residency, internship. She had scrimped and saved throughout their twelve-year marriage to help pay off his student loans, had run the household virtually alone during that time as he worked to establish his career, had tried time and again to bridge the increasing chasm between them as he focused on his practice to the complete exclusion of his family.

She had tried. Not perfectly, she would admit, but she had wanted her marriage to work.

Richard had had other ideas, though. He went to Paris for a conference and met his Giselle and decided family and vows and twelve years of marriage didn't stack up well against a twenty-year-old Frenchwoman with a tight body and pouty lips.

Jenny had long ago come to terms with Richard Boyer's betrayal of her. But she would never forgive him for what his complete abandonment of his family had done to his children. Morgan had stopped crying herself to sleep some time ago and seemed to be adjusting, but Cole carried so much anger inside him he seethed with it.

Lucky her, she seemed to be the only outlet for his rage.

She tried to remember what the therapist she'd seen in Seattle had told her, that Cole only lashed out at her because she was a safe target. Her son knew she wouldn't abandon him like his father, so he focused all the force of his rage toward her.

She still wasn't sure she completely bought into that explanation. Even if she did, she wasn't sure it would make his rebelliousness and unhappiness any more palatable.

With each mile marker, he seemed to sink further into gloom on the seat beside her.

A large timber arch across a gravel side road proudly bore the name of the Cold Creek Land & Cattle Company in cast-iron letters. She slowed the SUV and turned in.

"It won't be so bad," she said, fighting the completely juvenile urge to cross her fingers. "Who knows? You might even enjoy it."

He rolled his eyes. "Cleaning up horse crap? Right. Can't wait."

She sighed, wondering if Seth Dalton had any clue what joy was in store for him today.

The ranch house was shielded from the main road by a long row of trees, which made the first sight of it all the more dramatic. It was perfect for the landscape here, a bold, impressive structure of rock and logs, with the massive peaks of the Tetons as a backdrop.

She'd always considered November a particularly lonely, unattractive month, without October's swirling colors or December's sparkling anticipation. In November, the trees were bleak and bare and everything seemed frost-dead and barren.

The Cold Creek seemed to be an exception. Oh, the gardens out front had been cut down, the beds prepared for winter, but the long rows of weathered fence line and the sheer impressiveness of the house and outbuildings gave a stark beauty to the scene.

Not sure quite where to go to find Seth Dalton, she slowed as she reached the house and then stopped altogether when she saw a figure emerge from an immense barn, carrying a bale of hay by the baling twine.

It wasn't Seth, she realized, but his brother Wade, Natalie's father.

The oldest Dalton brother had two children in her school—Natalie and her younger brother, Tanner. Natalie was a dear, though a little bossy, but Tanner had been in her office on more than one occasion for some mischief or other. He wasn't malicious, just highly energetic.

The few times she had met with Wade Dalton and his wife, Caroline, at various school functions and when having discussions about Tanner's behavior, she'd been struck by the deep vein of happiness she sensed running through the family.

She didn't like to admit she felt envy and regret when she saw two people so obviously in love.

Wade caught sight of them now and smiled, dropping the bale and tipping his hat in a way she still hadn't become accustomed to here in cowboy country.

He didn't look at all surprised to see them as he crossed the yard to her SUV. Seth must have told him the whole story about Cole stealing his brother's car. What must he think of her and her delinquent son? she wondered, her face warming.

He only smiled in welcome. "Ms. Boyer. Kids," he said in that slow drawl she'd noticed before. "Welcome to the Cold Creek."

She couldn't help but smile back. "Thank you. We were supposed to be meeting your brother Seth this morning."

"Right. He mentioned your boy would be coming by to help him. He's up at the horse barn. Just follow the gravel road there another half mile or so and you can't miss it."

"Thank you," she said, wondering how big the ranch must be if the horse barn was a half mile from the main ranch house. The road took them up a slight grade, through a heavy stand of spruce and pines and aspen and then the view opened up and she caught sight of the horse operation.

Two dozen horses grazed in the vast pasture, their coats gleaming in the cool morning sunlight.

Barn seemed a vast understatement for the imposing white-painted structure that dominated the view. It was massive, at least twice as large as the barn they had passed closer to the ranch house, and more horses were in individual corrals off it.

As she pulled up and parked, she caught sight of a small two-story log home behind it. Situated to face the Tetons, the house had one steep gable with a balcony protruding from a window in the center and a wide porch looking out over the view.

She wasn't sure how she knew—maybe the tiny saplings out front that looked like they hadn't been there long—but the house looked new. Everything did, she thought. From the corrals to the vast gleaming barn to the pickup truck parked outside, everything gleamed with prosperity.

She had barely turned off the engine when Seth Dalton walked out of the barn and she had to catch her breath at the picture he made. He was wearing a worn denim jacket and a black cowboy hat. As he moved with that unconscious grace she'd noticed the night before, she saw he also wore figure-hugging jeans that suddenly made her feel jittery and weak-kneed.

The man was entirely too good-looking. She wasn't sure why that observation made her so irritable, but she found herself fighting the urge to shut the SUV door with a little more force than necessary, especially when he aimed that killer grin in her direction.

"Morning. It's a gorgeous one, isn't it?"

She raised a skeptical eyebrow. Clouds hung low over the Tetons and the cold wind felt heavy with the promise of snow.

"If you say so."

He laughed, a low, throaty sound that made her insides flutter, then he turned his attention to Cole, who had climbed out the other side of the vehicle to slouch against the door.

"You ready to work?"

Cole glowered at his benefactor, much to Jenny's chagrin. "Do I have a choice?"

In answer, Dalton just gave him a long, slow look and Jenny was amazed to watch Cole be the first to back down, shifting his gaze to the work boots he'd borrowed from his grandfather.

Before she could say anything, Seth's attention shifted to Morgan, who had climbed out of the backseat to join them.

"And who are you?"

"I'm Morgan Jeanette Boyer." She spoke with formal precision and held out her hand exactly like a nine-year-old princess greeting her favorite courtier.

A muscle twitched in Seth's cheek but he hid any sign of amusement as he took her hand and shook it. "Pleased to meet you, Miss Boyer. I'm Seth Dalton."

Morgan smiled. "I know. You're my friend Natalie's uncle. She says you have more girlfriends than Colin Farrell."

"Morgan!" Jenny exclaimed hotly, her cheeks fiery.

"What?" her daughter asked, all innocence.

Seth grinned, though Jenny thought she saw a hint of embarrassment behind it.

"Are all those horses your very own?" Morgan asked.

"Actually, most of them aren't. I have six or seven of my own but the rest I guess you could say I share with my family. Plus I'm training a few for other people."

He studied the avid interest in her eyes. "I don't suppose you'd want to have a look around, would you?"

Morgan gave a little jump of excitement. "Yeah! Can I, Mom?"

How could she say no? "I suppose. As long as you're sure we won't be in the way."

"Not at all. I have to show Cole around, anyway. No reason you two can't tag along."

They made a peculiar tour group, she thought as Seth led them inside the barn. It was more arena than stable, she realized. Though stalls ran around the perimeter, most of the space was taken up by a vast, open dirt floor. Handy for year-round training during the Idaho winters, she thought.

As he pointed out various features of the facility, Cole slouched along behind, Morgan asked a million questions and Jenny mainly focused on trying to keep her gaze away from Seth Dalton, difficult though it was.

"Everything looks so new," Jenny commented while Morgan was busy patting a horse and Cole slumped against the fence ringing the arena, looking as though he'd rather be anywhere else on the planet.

"The Cold Creek has been here for five generations, but the horse operation is pretty new. My brother and I decided a few years ago to diversify. We've always raised and trained our own horses on a limited scale and only for ourselves. We decided a few years ago to expand that part of our operations and try the open market."

"How has it been going?"

"I've got more work than I can handle right now."

"That's a good thing, isn't it?"

"Better than I ever dreamed." His smile was slow and sexy and seemed to suck all the oxygen molecules from the vast structure.

She didn't realize she was staring at it for several seconds, then she quickly shifted her gaze away from his mouth to find him watching her, an odd, glittery look in his blue eyes.

"What's that room?" Morgan asked, shattering the sudden painfully awkward silence.

Seth shifted his attention to her. "That's my office. Come on, I'll show you."

He opened the door to a small room several degrees warmer than the rest of the barn. When he opened the door, an oddly colored puppy blinked at them then jumped up from a blanket on the floor and started yipping a frantic greeting.

"You're finally waking up, sleepyhead?" Seth smiled at the pup. "Come and meet our company."

The puppy sniffed all their shoes in turn and made it

as far as Morgan before the girl scooped him up and hugged him tightly. "He's so cute! What's his name?"

"He's a she and her name is Lucy."

"Oh, you are a pretty girl. Yes you are," Morgan cooed, rubbing noses with the puppy. Jenny felt a pang. Her daughter adored animals of all shapes and sizes and used to constantly beg for a dog or cat of her own, until her pulmonologist in Seattle recommended against it.

"What kind of dog is she?" Cole asked, his first words since they'd arrived at the ranch.

"Australian shepherd. I bought her and her brother at a horse auction in Boise last month. I only meant to buy one for a birthday present for my mother but I couldn't resist Lucy."

"You have sheep, too?" Morgan asked.

"Uh, no." He looked a little embarrassed. "But they work cattle, too, and I figured she can help me when I'm training a horse for cutting."

"Cutting what?" Morgan asked.

"Cutting cattle. That's a term for picking an individual cow or calf out of a herd. A well-trained cutting horse will do all the work for a cowboy. He just has to point out which cow he wants and the horse will separate him out of the rest of the cows."

"Wow! Can your horses do that?"

Instead of being put off my Morgan's relentless questions, Seth seemed charmed by her daughter. "Some of them," he said. "Sometime when you come out I'll give you a demonstration."

"Cool!"

He grinned at Morgan's enthusiasm and Jenny could swear she felt her blasted knees wobble. Oh, the man was dangerous. Entirely too sexy for his own good. She had to get out of there before she dissolved into a brainless puddle of hormones.

"Morgan, you and I had better go. Cole and Mr. Dalton have work to do."

She was pleasantly surprised when Morgan didn't kick up a fuss but followed her out of the barn into the cool November sunshine. Only as they approached the SUV did Jenny pick up on the reason for her daughter's unusual docility.

In just a few seconds, Morgan had turned pale, her breathing wheezy and labored.

She should have expected it from the combination of animal dander, hay and excitement, but the swiftness of the asthma flare-up took her by surprise.

Still, Jenny had learned from grim experience never to go anywhere unprepared. She yanked the door open and lunged for her purse on the floor by the driver's seat. Inside was Morgan's spare inhaler and she quickly, efficiently puffed the medicine into the chamber and handed it to Morgan, then set her on the passenger seat while she drew the medicine into her lungs.

Morgan had that familiar panicky look in her eyes and Jenny spoke softly to calm her, the same nonsense words she always used.

She forgot all about Seth Dalton until he leaned past her into the SUV, big and disconcertingly masculine.

"That's it, honey," Seth said, keeping his own voice low and soothing. "Concentrate on the breathing and all the good air going into your lungs. You're doing great."

After a moment, the rescue medication did its work and the color started to return to her features. The panic in her eyes slowly gave way to the beginnings of relief and Jenny's heart twisted with pain for her child's trials and the courage Morgan wielded against them.

"Better?" Seth asked after a moment.

The girl nodded and Seth was grateful to see the flare-up seemed to be under control. "I'd tell you to go on back into the barn where it's warmer," he said to Jenny, "but I suspect the hay or the puppy triggered the attack, didn't they?"

Her eyes widened as if surprised he knew anything about asthma. He didn't tell her he could have written the damn book on it.

"That's what I thought," Jenny said. She was starting to lose her tight, in-control look, he saw, and now just looked like a worried mother. "I should have realized they might."

"Why don't we take her into the house over there for a minute until she feels better? This cold can't be the greatest for her lungs."

She looked as if she wanted to argue, but Morgan coughed just then and her mother nodded. "That's probably a good idea."

Seth scooped the girl into his arms easily, and headed for the house with Jenny and Cole following behind him. Morgan still breathed shallowly, her little chest rising and falling quickly as she tried to ease the horrible breathlessness he remembered all too well.

"I hate having asthma," she whispered, her voice far too bitter for a little girl.

He recognized the bitterness, too. He knew just what it felt like to be ten and trapped with a body that didn't work like he wanted it to. He had wanted to be a junior buckaroo rodeo champion, wanted to climb the Tetons by the time he was twelve, wanted to be the star pitcher on the Little League baseball team. Instead, he'd been small and weak and spent far too much time breathing into a lousy tube.

"Sucks, doesn't it?" he answered. "The worst is the one time you forget to take your inhaler somewhere and of course you suddenly you get hit by a flare-up."

She blinked at him and he was struck by how sweet it was to have a child look at him with such trust. "You have it, too?"

He nodded. "I don't have attacks very often now, maybe once or twice a year and they're usually pretty mild. When I was your age, though, it was a different story."

He set her down on his leather sofa and grabbed a blanket for her.

She couldn't seem to get over the fact that he knew what she was going through. "But you're big! You ride horses and everything."

"You can ride horses, too. You just have to watch for your triggers, like I do, and do your best to manage things. When I was a kid, they didn't have some of the newer maintenance meds they have now and we had a tough time finding the best treatment for me but eventually we did. You probably know you never grow out of asthma, but lots of times the symptoms decrease a lot when you get older. That's what happened to me."

"You probably weren't afraid like I am when I have an attack. Cole says I'm a big wussy."

Jenny looked pained by the admission and Seth sent the boy a pointed look. At least Cole had the grace to look embarrassed.

"I was just kidding," the kid mumbled. He needed a serious attitude adjustment, Seth thought, wondering if he'd been such a punk when he'd gone through his rebellious teens.

"I can't think of anything scarier than not being able to breathe," Seth told Morgan. "People who haven't been through it don't quite understand what it's like, do they? Like you're trapped underwater and somebody's got two fists around your lungs and is squeezing them tight so you can only take a tiny breath at a time."

Morgan nodded her agreement. "I always feel like I'm trapped under a big heavy blanket."

"What's your peak flow?"

She told him and he nodded. "Mine was pretty close to that when I was about your age." He paused and saw the conversation was starting to tire her. "Can I get you a glass of water or some juice?"

She nodded, closing her eyes, and he rose and went into the kitchen to find a glass. Somehow he wasn't surprised when Jenny followed him.

"Thank you." She gave him a quiet smile and he felt an odd little tug in his chest.

"I didn't do anything," he said as he poured a glass of orange juice from the refrigerator.

"You were very kind to her and I appreciate your sharing your own condition with her. It's great for Morgan to talk to adults who have managed to move past their childhood asthma and go on to live success-ful lives. Thank you," she said again, following it up this time with another small, hesitant smile.

He studied that smile, the way it highlighted the lushness of a mouth that seemed incongruous with her buttoned-down appearance.

What was it about her? She wasn't gorgeous in a Miss Rodeo Idaho kind of way. Not tall and curvy with a bril-liant smile and eyes that knew just how to reel a man in.

She was small and compact, probably no bigger than five foot three. He supposed he'd call her cute, with that red-gold hair and her green eyes and the little ski jump of a nose.

Seth couldn't say he had a particular favorite type of woman—he was willing to admit he loved them all—but he usually gravitated toward the kind of women who hung out at the Bandito. The kind in tight jeans and tighter shirts, with big breasts and hungry smiles.

Jenny Boyer was just about the polar opposite of that kind of woman. Cute or not, he probably wouldn't usually take a second look at a woman who looked like a suburban soccer mom, with her tailored tan slacks and her wool blazer. Jenny Boyer was the kind of settled, respectable woman men like him usually tended to avoid.

Yet here they were, and he couldn't seem to keep his eyes off her. She might not be his usual type but he sure liked looking at her.

He frowned a little at the unexpectedness of his attraction to her, then decided to shrug it off. He would never do anything about it. Not with a woman like Jenny Boyer, who had *Complication* written all over her.

Morgan's color was much better when they returned to the living room. She was sitting up bickering with her brother, something he figured was a good sign.

She took the juice from him with a shy smile.

"Cole and I have things to do but you two are welcome to hang out here until Morgan feels better."

"I think I'm all right now," the girl said.

"I should get her home for a nebulizer treatment and to check her peak flow."

"I can carry you back out to the car if you want."

Morgan shook her head. "I can walk. But thanks."

After her daughter was settled in the SUV, Jenny turned to him and to Cole.

"What time shall I come back?" she asked.

He thought of his schedule for the day. "Don't worry about it. I'll be running into town about four. We should be done by then so I'll bring him back and save you a trip. Just take care of Morgan."

"All right. Thank you." She looked at her son as if she wanted to say something more, but she only let out a long breath, slid into her vehicle and drove away.

"So are we going to work on the car or what?" Cole finally addressed him after the SUV pulled away.

If Seth hadn't noticed how concerned the boy had looked during those first few moments of the flare-up, he would probably find him more trouble than he was worth.

"Oh, eventually," he said with a smile that bordered on evil. "First, you've got some stalls to muck. I hope you brought good thick gloves because you're going to need 'em."

Chapter Three

Fourteen was a miserable bitch of an age.

Though more than half his life had passed since that notable year, it felt just as fresh and painful now as Seth watched Cole Boyer shovel manure out of a stall.

Though the kid wasn't tall by any stretch of the imagination, he was gangly and awkward, as if his muscles were still too short to keep up with his longer bones.

Seth remembered those days. He'd been small for his age, too, six inches shorter than most of the other guys in his class, and with asthma to boot. His father's death had been just a few years earlier. And while he hadn't been exactly paralyzed by grief over the bastard, he *had* struggled to figure out his place in the world now that he wasn't Hank Dalton's sickly, sissy-boy youngest son.

He'd been a little prick, too, full of anger and attitude. He had brothers to pound on to help vent some of it, but since fights usually ended with them beating the tar out of him, he tended to shy away from that activity. Eventually, he'd turned some of his excess energy to horses.

He trained his first horse that year, he remembered, a sweet little chestnut mare he'd ridden in the Idaho state high school rodeo finals a few years later.

Yeah, fourteen had been miserable, for the most part. But the next year everything started to come together. Between his fourteenth and fifteenth years, he hit a major growth spurt, the asthma all but disappeared and he gained six inches of height and thirty pounds of muscle, almost as if his body had just been biding its time.

Girls who'd ignored him all his life suddenly sat up and took notice—and he noticed them right back. After that, adolescence became a hell of a lot more fun, though he doubted Jenny Boyer would appreciate him sharing that particular walk down memory lane with her son, no matter how miserable he looked about life right now.

He *should* be miserable, Seth thought. Though he was tempted to turn soft and tell Cole he'd done enough for the day, he only had to think about the damage to his GTO to stiffen his resolve.

A little misery never hurt a kid.

"Can you hurry it up here?" Seth leaned indolently on the stall railing, mostly because he knew it would piss the kid off.

Sure enough, all he earned for his trouble was a heated glare.

"This isn't exactly easy."

"It's not supposed to be," Seth said.

After three hours, the kid had only mucked out four stalls, with two more to go. The more he shoveled, the grimmer his mood turned, until Seth was pretty sure he was ready to implode.

Tempted as he was to wait for the explosion, he finally took pity on him and reached for another shovel.

Cole gave him a surprised look when Seth joined him in the stall. "I thought I was supposed to be doing this."

"You are. But since I'd like to take a look at the car you trashed sometime today, I figure the only way that's going to happen is if I lend a hand."

"I'm going as fast as I can," Cole muttered.

"I know. If I thought you were slacking, you can bet I'd still be out there watching."

Surprise flickered in eyes the same green as his mother's, but he said nothing. They worked in silence for a few moments, the only sounds the scrape of shovels on concrete, the whickers of the horses around them and Lucy's curious yips as she followed them.

Only after they'd moved onto the last stall did the boy speak. "Why don't you have a real job or something?" he asked, his tone more baffled than hostile.

Seth raised an eyebrow. "You don't think this is real work?"

"Sure. But what kind of loser signs up to shovel horse crap all day?"

Seth laughed. "If this was the only thing I did around here all day, I'd have to agree with you. But I usually leave the grunt work to the hired help while I get to do the fun stuff."

"Like what?"

"Working with the horses. Breeding them, training them."

"Whatever."

"Not a real horse fan?"

"They're big and dumb. How hard could it be to train them?"

"You might be surprised." He scraped another shovel

full of sunshine. "I can tell you there's nothing so satisfying as taking a green-broke horse—that means an untrained one—and working with him until he obeys anything you tell him to do without question."

"Whatever," Cole said again, his voice dripping with scorn.

To his surprise, Seth found he was more amused by the kid's attitude than he'd been by anything in a long time. "Come on. I'll show you. Drop your shovel."

Cole didn't need a second invitation. He dropped it with a clatter and followed Seth toward a stall at the end of the row, where his big buckskin Stella waited.

In moments, he had her saddled, then led her outside to one of the corrals where he kept a dozen or so cattle to help with the training.

"Okay, now pick a steer."

"Why?"

He had to laugh at the boy's horrified expression. "I'm not going to make you ride the thing, I promise. Remember how I was telling Morgan about cutting? Stella's going to cut whatever steer you pick out of the herd for you. Just tell me which one you want her to go after."

"How the hell should I know? They all look the same!"

"You've got a lot to learn, city boy. How about the one in the middle there, with the white face?"

At least the kid had lost his belligerence, though he was looking at Seth like he'd been kicked by a horse one too many times.

"Sure. Get that one."

He gave the commands to Stella then sat back in the saddle and let her do her thing. She was brilliant, as usual. In minutes, she had the white-faced Hereford just where Seth wanted him, away from the herd and heading for the fence where Cole had perched to watch the demonstration.

"There you go. He's all yours," Seth called over the cattle's lowing.

The boy jumped down faster than a bullet at the sight of a half-ton animal heading toward him.

Seth pulled Stella off and let the steer return to the rest of the herd, then led the horse back through the gate.

"So what do you think? She's brilliant, isn't she?"

"You told her what to do."

"Sure. But she did it, didn't she? Without even hesitating. She's a great horse." He slid out of the saddle, then sent the kid a sidelong glance. "You do much riding?"

Cole snorted. "There aren't too many horses on Seattle street corners sitting around waiting to be ridden."

"You don't have that excuse here. Get on."

Before Cole could argue, Seth handed him the reins and hefted him into the saddle.

He looked even smaller than his age up on the big horse, though Seth gave him points for not sliding right back down. With one hand on the bridle, he led them back inside the training facility.

"You probably know the basics, even if you've never ridden before, just from watching TV. Keep a firm hand on the reins, pull them in the direction you want her to go. Above all, have fun."

He let go of the bridle, confident the horse was too well-trained to unseat her rider, no matter how inexperienced.

Sure enough, she started a slow walk around the arena. Cole looked terrified at first, then he gradually started to relax. By the second time around the arena, he even smiled a little, though he bounced in the saddle like a particularly hapless sack of flour.

"I suck, don't I?" he said ruefully as they passed Seth.

Sit up, boy. Or are you too tired *to learn to be a man?*

*You'll never be able to ride the damn thing if you slouch
in the saddle like that and gasp like a trout on the end
of a frigging hook every time the horse takes a step.*

He pushed away the echo of his father's voice, wondering if he'd been four or five during that particular
riding lesson. "You don't suck," he assured Seth. "You
just have to learn to move with the rhythm of the horse.
It takes a while to figure it out. For your first time,
you're kickin' A."

For one shining instant, Cole looked thrilled at the
praise. He must have felt himself smile, though, because
he quickly retreated back into his brittle shell.

"Am I done here? My butt's starting to hurt."

Seth sighed as the momentary animation slipped
away. He shrugged and held Stella again so Cole could
slide down.

"We've got one more stall to finish. Work on that
while I take off Stella's saddle."

Cole grimaced but headed back to his shovel.

He couldn't expect to change the kid's attitude with
one horseback ride, Seth thought. But maybe the car
would do the trick.

He caught his own thoughts and grimaced at himself.
Since when was he the do-gooder of Pine Gulch? He
had no business even trying to fix this troubled kid's
problems. Better just to get his money's worth out of
him in labor to compensate for the car damage and leave
the attitude-adjusting to his mother.

Saturdays were usually one of her most productive
days of the week, away from the office and all the dis-
tractions of running an elementary school with four
hundred students.

She usually accomplished more in a few hours than

she could do in two days at school, between lunch duty and phone calls from concerned parents and dealing with state and federal education regulations.

Today, Jenny couldn't seem to focus on work at all while she waited for Seth Dalton to return with Cole.

After trying for an hour and a half to slog through some paperwork while Morgan rested on the couch next to her in the den watching television, she finally gave it up for a lost cause.

She wasn't worried about Cole. Not precisely. She was more concerned that her belligerent son would forget Seth was doing him a huge favor and instead would vent his unhappiness in all the usual ways.

She couldn't stress about that. Something told her a man like Dalton was more than capable of holding his own against a fourteen-year-old rebel.

He struck her as a man who could handle just about anything. She thought of those strong, capable shoulders and had to suppress a sigh. Why couldn't she seem to get the man off her mind?

She'd had an unwilling fascination for him since the first time she heard his name, long before her son's recklessness brought them into his orbit. It had been a month or so after school started and she'd been in her office after lunch when one of her brand-new teachers, just out of college and still half terrified of her students, stopped in during her prep hour to talk to Marcy, the school secretary.

It hadn't surprised her the two were friends. Marcy was only a few years older than Ashley Barnes, the new kindergarten teacher. Beyond that, she was warm and bubbly, the kind of person who drew everyone to her. Not only was she great at her job but the children adored her and Jenny had learned most of the other teachers did, too.

She hadn't meant to eavesdrop, but her door had been open and she'd been able to hear every word.

"He said he'd call me," Ashley complained. "How stupid was I to believe him?"

Marcy had only laughed. "You're human and you're female. There's not a woman in town who can resist Seth Dalton when he gives that smile of his. Heck, he even has all the old ladies in my grandma's quilting club batting their fake eyelashes at him."

"That night at the Bandito, you'd think I was the only woman in the world," Ashley said, the bitterness in her voice completely at odds with her usual sunny disposition. "He never left my side all night and we danced every single dance. I thought he really liked me."

"I'm sure he did like you that night. But that's the thing about Seth. He lives completely in the moment."

"He's a dog." Ashley sounded close to tears.

"No he's not. Believe it or not, he's actually a pretty decent guy. He's the first one out on his tractor plowing his neighbors' driveways after a big snowstorm and he always stops to help somebody in trouble. But he was blessed—or cursed, however you want to look at it— with the kind of good looks that make women go a little crazy around him."

"You think I imagined that night?"

"No. Oh, honey, I'm sure you didn't," Marcy had replied in her patient, kind voice. "My friends and I have a theory. We call it Seth Dalton's School of Broncobustin'. If you're lucky to find him turning his attention to you, just climb on and hold on tight. It probably won't last too long, but it will be a hell of a ride."

"I'm not like that!" Ashley had exclaimed. "I never even go to bars. I don't drink. I probably wouldn't even have met him if my roommate hadn't dragged me along that night."

"Which is probably the reason he didn't call you," Marcy pointed out gently. "You're a kindergarten teacher with *Marriage Material* stamped on your forehead. You're sweet and innocent, and you probably have already got names picked out for the four kids you're going to have."

"Is that such a bad thing?"

"Oh, honey, absolutely not. I think it's wonderful, and somewhere out there is someone who is going to love those things about you. But that's not what Seth Dalton is about."

One of the third-graders had come in just then complaining of a stomach ache. Marcy had turned her attention to calling the girl's mother to come get her and Ashley had returned to her class, but not before Jenny had developed a strong dislike for the man under discussion.

It was one of those weird cases where, once she heard a name, she suddenly couldn't seem to escape it: Seth Dalton's kept popping up.

She heard another teacher just before the start of a faculty meeting talk about running into him in the grocery store and how she'd been so flustered just because he'd smiled and asked her how she was that she'd left without half the items on her list.

When they were brainstorming ways to raise money for new library books, someone suggested a bachelor auction and someone else said they'd have enough books to fill every shelf if only they could get Seth Dalton on the auction block.

Now that she'd met him, she certainly understood all the buzz about the man. A woman could forget her own name just from one look out of those blue eyes.

"Are you done with your work?" Morgan asked from her spot on the couch, distracting her from her completely unproductive train of thought.

She closed her laptop and gathered her papers, shoving them back into her briefcase. She had learned long ago how to recognize a lost cause. "For now. Want to watch a DVD or play a game?"

"Sure. You pick."

They were still discussing their options a moment later when she heard the back door open and a moment later her father came in, his cheeks red from the November chill and his arms full of wood to replenish the low supply in the firebox by the woodstove.

"You should let me do that," she chided, upset at herself for being too distracted by thoughts of Seth Dalton to pay attention to her father's activities.

"Why?" Jason looked genuinely surprised.

"I feel guilty sitting here where it's warm and comfortable while you're outside hauling wood."

"I need the exercise. Keeps my joints lubricated."

She had to laugh at that. At sixty-five, her father was more fit than most men half his age. He rode his mountain bike all over town, he fished every chance he got—winter or summer—and his new passion was cross-country skiing.

"Maybe I need the exercise, too."

"And maybe it does my heart good to know I'm still capable of seeing to the comfort of my daughter and granddaughter. You wouldn't want to take that away from an old man, would you?" Jason said, with a twinkle in his eyes and the incontrovertible logic that had made him such a formidable opponent in the courtroom.

She rolled her eyes and was amused to see Morgan copying her gesture.

"Grandpa, you're silly," her daughter said with fondness. "You're not old."

The two of them were kindred spirits and got along like the proverbial house on fire. Coming to Pine Gulch had been the right decision, she thought again. Even if Cole still fought and bucked against it like one of Seth Dalton's horses with a burr under the saddle, the move had been good for all of them.

She couldn't be sorry for it. Morgan and Cole had come to know the grandfather they had been acquainted with only distantly, and in a lot of ways, Jenny felt the same. Jason had been a distant, distracted figure in her life, even before her parents had divorced when she was twelve. Coming here had led to a closer relationship than they'd ever had.

"We're going to watch a DVD. Are you interested? We're debating between a *Harry Potter* or one of the *Lord of the Rings* trilogy."

"Oh, Tolkien. By all means."

They settled on which of the three to see and were watching the opening credits when by some mother's intuition, she heard the low rumble of a truck out front.

"Go ahead and start the movie," she said. "Since I've seen it at least a dozen times, I'm sure I won't be too lost when I come back."

She reached the front door just as Cole hopped down from a big silver pickup truck. Through the storm door, she studied her son intently. Though he didn't appear to be exactly overflowing with joy, he didn't seem miserable, either, as he headed up the sidewalk to the house.

She wasn't really surprised when Seth climbed out the other side of the truck and followed the boy up to the house. She opened the door for her son, who would probably have walked right by without even a greeting if she hadn't stepped right in his way.

"How did it go?" she asked, fighting the yearning to pull him into her arms for the kind of hug he used to give her all the time.

"My favorite Levi's smell like horse crap."

"I'm sure that will wash out."

"I doubt it," Cole grumbled. "They're probably ruined forever."

"Here's a tip for you," Seth spoke from the doorway with a lazy smile. "Next time you come to the ranch, maybe you shouldn't wear your favorite pair of Levi's."

"If you're going to suggest I buy a pair of Wranglers, I might just have to puke."

"I wouldn't dare," Seth drawled. "Then your favorite pair of Levi's would smell like horse crap and puke."

Cole's snort might have passed for a laugh, but Jenny could not be quite sure.

"Wear whatever you want. But if you take the school bus to the Cold Creek on Tuesday, we might be ready to get into the real work on the car now that we've taken a look at the damage. Bus Fifteen is the one you want to take. Ray Pullman is the driver."

"Right. I need to take a shower."

"Bring your jeans out when you're done so we can wash them," Jenny said.

Cole didn't answer her or even acknowledge her as he headed down the stairs to his bedroom, leaving her alone with Seth.

In part because of embarrassment over her son's rudeness and in part because Seth was so masculine and so blasted attractive, she was intensely aware of him. He seemed to fill up all the available space in the small foyer.

She gave a small huff of annoyance at herself and tried to ignore the scent of him that seemed to surround her, of warm male and sexy aftershave.

"Tell me the truth. How did it really go today? I doubt Cole will tell me much."

"Good. He worked hard at everything I asked him to do and some of it wasn't very appealing. I can't ask for more than that."

She relaxed the fingers she hadn't realized she'd clenched tightly in the pockets of her sweater. "Was he…" her voice trailed off and she couldn't figure out how to ask the question in a way that wouldn't make her sound like a terrible mother.

"Rude and obnoxious? Not much, surprisingly. He digs cars and we spent much of the afternoon working on mine, so everything was cool."

"I can't tell you how relieved that makes me."

"You should probably know I did throw him up on a horse for a few minutes. He actually seemed to enjoy it. Even smiled a few times."

She blinked, trying to imagine her rebellious city-boy "I-hate-everything-country" son on the back of a horse.

"You're sure we're talking about the same kid? He wasn't possessed by alien cowboy pod people?"

Seth laughed, his blue eyes crinkled at the corners, and she could swear she felt warm fingers trickling down her spine just looking at him.

"Not a UFO in sight, I swear."

She shouldn't be here, sharing laughter or anything else with Seth Dalton. With sharp efforts, she broke eye contact. "Thank you for all the trouble you've gone to," she said after an uncomfortable moment. "It would have been less work on your part if you had just turned him over to the authorities."

"I'm getting free labor with my horses and with my car. Not a bad deal. I'm no saint here."

"So they tell me."

Had she really said that aloud? She mentally cringed at her rudeness and Seth looked startled at first, then gave her one of those blasted slow smiles that ought to come with a warning label as long as her arm.

"Who's been talking about me, Ms. Boyer?"

Her nerve endings tingled at his low, amused voice, but she ignored it, turning her own voice prim. "Who hasn't? You're a favorite topic of conversation in Pine Gulch, Mr. Dalton."

He didn't seem bothered by town gossip—or maybe he was just used to it.

Looking for all the world as if he planned to make himself right at home, he leaned a hip against the door frame and crossed his arms across his chest. "That must tell you what a quiet town you've settled in, if nobody in Pine Gulch has anything more interesting to talk about than me. So what's the consensus?"

That you're a major-league player. That you flirt with anything female and have left a swath of broken hearts behind you. That half the women in Teton Valley are in love with you and the other half are in lust.

She *so* didn't want to be having this conversation with him. She thought longingly of the paperwork she'd been putting off all afternoon and would have given just about anything right then to be sitting at her desk filling out federal assessment forms. Anything but this.

"Nothing I'm sure you haven't already heard," she finally said. "You're apparently a busy man."

A purely masculine, absolutely enticing dimple appeared in his cheek briefly then disappeared again.

"Yeah, starting a full-fledged horse ranch can take a lot of hours."

He had to know she wasn't talking about his equine endeavors, but she decided she wasn't going to set him straight.

"I'm sure it does," she murmured drily. Dating a different woman every night probably tended to fill up the calendar, too. But not this woman, even if she wasn't four years older than him and the exact opposite of all the tight, perky young things he was probably used to.

She knew all about men like him. She'd been married to one, a man compelled to charm every woman in sight.

She had worked hard to rebuild her heart and her life and her family in the last three years. After a great deal of hard work and self-scrutiny, she had finally become someone she could respect again.

She was a strong, successful woman who loved her work and her family, and she wasn't about to let a man like Seth Dalton knock her on her butt again.

Even if he did make her hormones wake up and sing hallelujah.

"Thank you for taking the time away from your horses to bring Cole back," she said, in what she hoped was a polite but dismissive tone.

He either didn't pick on it or didn't care. "No problem. How's Morgan doing now?"

She didn't want him to be interested in her daughter or for the simple question to remind her just how kind and patient he had been during Morgan's flare-up.

That was the problem with charmers, she supposed. They seemed instinctively to know how to zero in on a woman's weak spot and use that to their advantage. He'd already slipped inside her defenses a little by being so decent about Cole crashing his car. She would have preferred if he ignored Morgan altogether.

How was she to pigeonhole him as a selfish woman-izer when he showed such genuine concern for her daughter's welfare?

"She's fine. By the time we returned home, her peak flow was about seventy percent. After we nebulized her, it went up to about eight-five percent."

"Good. I hope the flare-up doesn't discourage you from bringing her out to the ranch again. She's welcome to tag along with Cole anytime. You both are."

She smiled politely, though she had absolutely no in-tention of taking him up on the invitation. "Thank you. But I'm sure the very last thing you need underfoot— with you being so *busy* and all—is a wheezing nine-year-old girl."

"I'd like to have her back. Both of you. Pretty ladies are always welcome at the Cold Creek."

His smile was designed to reach right into a woman's soul and she felt it clear to her toes. Darn him. No, darn her for this ridiculous crush, the weakness she had for handsome charmers.

She couldn't endure his light flirtation, especially knowing he didn't mean any of it, it was all just a game to him.

He couldn't possibly be seriously interested in a stuffy, overstressed thirty-six-year-old elementary school principal with no chest to speak of and the tiniest bit of gray in her hair that she only managed to hide by the grace of God and a good stylist.

He wasn't interested in her, and he had no business smiling at her as if he were.

"Do you stay up nights thinking of lines or do you just come up with them on the fly?"

He raised an eyebrow, though amusement still lurked in his blue eyes, even in the face of her frontal attack. "Was that a line? I thought I was simply extending an invitation."

She sighed. "Look, you've been incredibly understanding about what Cole did to your car. If I had been in your shoes, I can't imagine I would be nearly so magnanimous. He's going to be working with you to make things right for at least a few months and I suppose we'll see a great deal of each other in that time, so let's get this out of the way."

"I'm all ears."

And sexy smiles and gorgeous eyes and broad shoulders that look like they could carry the weight of the world.

She frowned at herself. "I'm not interested in being charmed," she said bluntly.

"Is that what you think I was doing?"

"Weren't you?" She didn't give him a chance to answer. "I doubt you're even aware of it, it's so ingrained in your nature. The flirting, the slow bedroom smiles. Even if you're not attracted to a woman, something in your blood compels you to conquer her, to find her weaknesses and exploit them until she surrenders to your charm like every other woman."

He gazed at her, obviously taken aback by the sudden attack. She heard her own rudeness and was appalled but couldn't seem to stop the words from gushing out.

All she could think of was Ashley Barnes crying her eyes out when Seth never called her back and Richard murmuring lies and promises while he was already sleeping with another woman and planning to abandon his children.

"It's different if a man is genuinely interested in a woman," she went on. "If he truly wants to know about her, if he might feel some spark of attraction and want to follow up on it. That's one thing. But you're not interested in me. Men like you charm just because you can."

He straightened from the door jamb, a sudden fiery light in his eyes that had her stepping back a pace. "That's quite a scathing indictment, Ms. Boyer, especially since you've known me less than a day. I thought good teachers and principals weren't supposed to rush to snap judgments."

His words gave her pause and she had to wonder what in heaven's name seemed to possess her around him.

"You're right. Absolutely. I'm very sorry. That was completely uncalled-for. I'll make a deal with you. I won't rush to any snap judgments provided you refrain from trying to add me to your list of conquests."

Before he could answer, she held open the door in a pointed dismissal. Cold air rushed in, swirling around her like a malicious fog, but she knew it wouldn't be enough to take care of her hot embarrassment. "Thank you again for bringing Cole home. I'll be sure to send him out to your ranch on the bus Tuesday."

Seth gave her a long, hard look, as if he had much more he wanted to say, but he finally turned around and walked outside.

She closed the door and leaned against it, her hands clenched at her sides.

How had she let him get her so stirred up? He hadn't done anything. Not really. Sure, he'd flirted a little, but she had always been able to handle a mild flirtation. He seemed to push all her buttons—and several she hadn't realized were there.

How on earth was she supposed to face him again after she'd all but accused him of trying to seduce her?

She would simply have to be cool and polite. She

would be gracious about what he was doing for her son but distant about everything else. She had no doubt she could keep him at arm's length, especially after she'd just slapped him down so firmly.

Keeping him out of her head was a different matter entirely.

Chapter Four

Seth stood on the porch of Jason Chambers's red-brick rambler, the November evening air sharp with fall, and tried to figure out what the heck had just happened in there.

He wasn't at all used to being on the receiving end of such a blunt dismissal, and he was fairly certain he didn't care for it much. He had only been talking to the woman, just trying to be friendly, and she was treating him like she'd just caught him looking up her skirt.

He wasn't quite sure how to react. He had certainly encountered his share of rejection. It never usually bothered him, not when there were so many other prospects out there.

He had to admit, he just wasn't used to rejection accompanied by such blatant hostility.

He ought to just march right back in there and ask Jenny Boyer what he had done in the course of their short acquaintance to warrant it. He lifted a hand to the doorbell then let it fall again.

No. What would that accomplish, besides making him look foolish? She had the right to her opinions, even if they were completely ridiculous.

Even if you're not attracted to a woman, something in your blood compels you to conquer her, to find her weaknesses and exploit them until she surrenders to your charm like every other woman.

That wasn't true. He didn't need to charm every female he came in contact with. He just happened to be a sociable kind of guy.

Where did she get off forming such a harsh opinion on him when they'd barely met?

More to the point, why did it bug him so much?

It was no big deal, he told himself as the cold wind slapped at him. Better to just forget about Ms. Uptight Jennifer Boyer and head over to the Bandito, where he could find any number of warm, willing women who didn't think he was so objectionable.

His boots thudded on the steps as he headed off the porch toward his truck. He climbed in and started the engine, but for some strange reason couldn't bring himself to drive away from the house just yet, too busy analyzing his own reaction to being flayed alive by a tongue sharper than his best Buck knife.

He ought to be seriously pissed off at the woman and not want anything more to do with her. He was, he told himself.

So why was he somehow even more attracted to her?

He liked curvy women who played up their assets, who wore low-cut blouses and short skirts and towering high heels that made their legs look long and sexy.

His brothers seemed to think that was just another

sign that he needed to grow up and get serious about life. He had to wonder what Jake and Wade would say if they knew about this strange attraction for the new elementary school principal.

Yeah, he liked looking at her—the tilt of her chin and the flash of her green eyes and those lush lips that seemed at odds with her starchy appearance.

And she smelled good. He had definitely picked up on that. Her perfume had been soft and sweet, putting all kinds of crazy images in his head of wildflowers and spring mountain rain showers.

And her hair. A man could go a little crazy trying to figure out just how to describe it. It was red, yeah, but not just red. Instead, it was a hundred different shades, from gold to something that reminded him of the first soft brush of color on the maples in fall.

He let out a breath. Oh, he was attracted to her all right. Curiously more so now than he'd been even before he walked inside with Cole.

More than that, he was also intensely curious to know whether he could change her opinion of him.

The challenge of it seemed irresistible suddenly.

He shook his head at himself, wholly aware of the irony. He was sitting here pondering how to change the mind of a woman who thought he was nothing more than a womanizer. That was all fine, except for the reason he wanted to change her mind—because he wanted to seduce her, exactly like the womanizer she thought he was.

He ought to just drive away and leave her alone. But the thought of that was as unappealing as riding a steer. He had to try. Something about her prim, buttoned-down beauty appealed to him more than any woman in longer than he could remember.

He didn't even want to think what insight someone could get into his brain that the first woman to really intrigue him in a long time was the one woman who apparently wanted nothing to do with him.

Was she right, that it was all about the challenge to him? Maybe.

But what was life without a little challenge?

Jennifer Boyer was a tough nut to crack, Seth thought two weeks later outside the Cold Creek horse barn.

He'd seen her a handful of times since that first evening when he dropped Cole off. Though he'd been tempted to pour on the charm, he decided on a more low-key approach. She told him she wasn't interested in a flirtation and he had a strong feeling she would automatically reject any blatant overtures so instead he had tried to be warm and friendly, carefully suppressing any sign of his increasing attraction.

Whatever he was doing wasn't working. She wasn't interested. Worse, she seemed more distant each time they met than she had the time before. She responded politely enough, all the while looking at him out of those green eyes that he discovered could turn to ice chips in an instant.

He should have given it up for a lost cause a week ago, but the more she pushed him away, the harder he tried to find a foothold. He was determined to change her mind about him, but after two weeks he was beginning to fear it was a lost cause.

The only chink in her hard shell appeared to be Lucy, he had discovered. The stiff, distant principal seemed to melt around his puppy. Her whole demeanor relaxed and her face lit up in a smile that took his breath away.

Though it was no doubt ruthless of him, he had to admit, he flaunted his single advantage without scruple.

He wasn't a stupid man—he always made sure Lucy was awake and nearby, looking her adorable self, whenever he knew Jenny was due to arrive at the ranch with Cole.

If nothing else, Lucy served the purpose of keeping his quarry around a little longer, when he was sure she would otherwise have rushed off in a second. She always seemed to be in a hurry to get somewhere, unless the puppy happened to be around.

He watched her and Morgan now tossing a ball for Lucy. The late-autumn sunlight glinted off that magnificent hair and she looked fresh and soft and beautiful.

He wanted her with a heat that continued to baffle him.

Morgan was the one throwing the ball, so by rights Lucy should have been returning it to her. But she couldn't seem to get the message and kept dropping it at Jennifer's feet, to the amusement of all of them.

"You silly girl. What are we going to do with you?" Jenny said after several repeats of the neat little trick he would have taught the puppy, if only he'd thought of it. She picked Lucy up and brushed noses with her and it was all he could do hide the naked longing he knew must be obvious on his face.

He turned his attention to Morgan instead. "You're really great with her. You ought to think about being a vet."

Morgan beamed at him with none of her mother's reserve. "That's just what I told my teacher I want to be! I wrote a paper about it in school. Me and Natalie both want to be veterinarians."

This was new. Last he heard, his niece wanted to be a rodeo queen, but then he figured Nat would probably change her mind a hundred more times before she even reached middle school.

He tugged at one of her ponytails. "Tell you what. The next time the vet is scheduled to come out to look at my horses for some reason on a weekend or holiday, I'll give you a call and you and Natalie can tag along and watch him. If it's all right with your mom, of course."

Morgan's face lit up, making him feel about a dozen feet tall. Now if only he could get her mother to look at him the same way....

"Oh, please, Mom!" she begged. "It would be so awesome to watch a vet work with real horses. We wouldn't get in the way, I swear."

Jenny didn't look thrilled to be put on the spot. "We'll have to see," she murmured in that cool, noncommittal tone every parent seemed to have perfected.

In his limited experience, a "We'll see" was just the same as a "No" but Morgan didn't seem to see it the same way. She looked ecstatic at the possibility. He wanted to tell her most of the time the vets just came out to give shots, not do anything exciting or dramatic, but he didn't want to spoil it for her.

The girl threw the ball for the puppy one more time just as Cole came out of the garage.

"Finished putting the tools away?" Seth asked.

The boy nodded. "You know, I bet she's looking better now than she ever has, even when she was new."

Seth laughed. "You might be right. I can't imagine the folks in Detroit took as much care building her as we've spent restoring her."

Cole grinned and held up his bandaged index finger, the result of a minor accident with a rough piece of metal. "And we've got the war wounds to prove it."

If Seth hadn't been watching Jenny, he might have missed the raw emotion on her face when she looked at her son.

"How's the work on the car coming?" she asked. Seth opened his mouth to answer but saw her gaze was still trained on her son so he waited for the boy to answer.

"Okay," Cole said. Though he spoke only a single word, his tone wasn't at all his usual surly one.

"Better than okay," Seth corrected. "We've got the minor dings smoothed out and we're waiting for a new headlamp we had to order from a specialty shop back East. Cole here is kicking butt on smoothing out the scrape on the side."

The boy looked pleased. "It's nothing. I'm only doing what you tell me to do."

"That's just what you're supposed to be doing," he growled. "Now if only I can keep you from throwing in those crappy CDs you call music, we'll get along fine."

"Just because you drive an old car doesn't mean you have to listen to the same music my grandpa does."

"It's blues and classic rock. And good for your grandpa, if he listens to CCR and Bob Seger. Maybe between the two of us, we can teach you to appreciate fine music."

Cole made a gagging sound that sent his sister into the giggles. Seth had to admit, for all his belligerence at first, the kid had warmed to him far easier than his mother had.

Cole Boyer loved cars. No question about it. Every time he walked into the garage to work on the GTO, he became a different kid. It was a physical and emotional change that Seth found fascinating to watch. He lifted his shoulders and stopped the perpetual slouch, he made eye contact more, he climbed out of his attitude and talked and chattered as much as Seth's nephew Tanner.

He glowed while he was working on the GTO and it was one more vivid reminder to Seth of himself. It didn't matter how small he'd been until he was fifteen, that he was wheezy and raspy and weak. Behind the wheel of a hot car, everything was relative.

Cole even seemed to respond to the horses. Every time he came to the ranch, Seth saddled a horse for him to ride a little. At first he hadn't been very enthusiastic about it, but as he gained more confidence in the saddle, that seemed to be changing.

Today Cole had even spurred his horse to a slight lope around the arena and had looked as thrilled by it as a bronc rider the first time he hit eight seconds on the timer.

He had to admit, he liked the kid. He was smart and worked hard. Though he still adopted his tough-guy attitude from time to time, when he relaxed his guard enough to let it slip, he was funny and bright and full of interesting observations about the world around him.

His favorite days of the week were those when Cole came out and helped him around the place—and only part of that had to do with knowing he would probably see Jenny, since she usually drove out to the Cold Creek to pick him up.

"When we have her back to her full glory, we'll all have to take a celebratory drive somewhere," Seth said. "Maybe we can run over to Idaho Falls for dinner or something."

"Can we take Lucy?" Morgan asked.

"If she learns to behave herself and doesn't pee on my floor mats."

Morgan giggled. "She is so cute. I wish we could take her home."

"You should see her with her brother," Seth said. "The two of them are quite a pair."

"Is he bossy, too?" Morgan asked him, with a pointed look at her own brother.

"I think she's the bossy one, but it's hard to tell. They wrestle and play and get into all kinds of mischief when they're together."

"I bet they're funny," Morgan said.

"Come on, kids," Jenny finally broke in. "I have another school board meeting tonight and I don't want to dump all the chores and homework on Grandpa to supervise."

"Can I throw one more time?" Morgan asked. "I know she'll bring it back to me this time."

An idea sparked in his head as he watched the girl with the puppy—who finally seemed to get it right and dropped the ball at her feet instead of Jenny's.

He discarded it at first as completely out of the question, but it seemed to rattle around in his head as Cole and Morgan were climbing into her little SUV. He didn't want her to feel backed into a corner so he waited until they were settled inside the car, out of earshot, before he spoke.

"Do you have plans tomorrow?"

She looked at him warily. "Why?"

"I know it's still a week before Thanksgiving but my family is getting together tomorrow to go up on some land we've got up in the mountains to cut Christmas trees. We try to do it a little early before the real heavy snows hit. Why don't you all come along? My mother and brothers will be here. I'm sure Mom will bring Linus so Morgan can have the chance to play with both of the puppies."

She blinked, clearly not expecting that kind of invitation from him.

"It's a lot of fun," he pressed, warming to the idea more and more. "We usually take sleds up and make a big party out of it. The kids would have a great time."

She pursed her lips. "I don't think so. It sounds like a family outing. I wouldn't want to intrude."

"You wouldn't be, I swear. Wade has already invited our vet and his family along and there's always room for a few more. I was up there on our land a month or so ago during round-up and tagged more than a dozen little spruces that would be perfect for Christmas trees. You only have to pick out your favorite and there are plenty to go around. You won't find fresher trees anywhere."

She looked tempted as she gazed up at the mountains. Her eyes softened and her expression turned wistful. What would he have to do to have her turn that kind of expression in his direction?

Right then he would have crawled up that mountain on his knees and ripped a tree out with his bare hands if it would make her look at *him* with those soft green eyes.

"Just think what a great holiday memory that would be for your kids," he pushed, wondering when he'd become so ruthless.

Jenny let out a breath at his words. Blast him. Seth Dalton could sell sunshine in the desert. She had been right about him that day at her father's house. The man knew just the right buttons to push, somehow instinctively finding exactly a woman's weakness and using it against her. How could he possibly know that she dreamed of creating the perfect holiday for her children?

She had such hopes for this year, wishing she could make up for the awful holidays past. The last few had been anything but pleasant as both children had been angry and upset after their father had broken yet more promises to visit.

Even before he'd left for Europe and completely abdicated his responsibility to his family, she'd been on her own most holidays. Richard often chose to work extra shifts during the holidays and Cole and Morgan saw him only sporadically.

Like Chevy Chase in Cole's favorite Christmas movie, she had dreamed about making this year perfect. They were in a new home, with a clean, blank slate for creating family traditions. And wouldn't riding into the mountains for their own tree be a perfect start?

Oh, she was tempted by his offer. Her mind was already conjuring up some Currier & Ives images of sleigh rides and hot cocoa and jingle bells on stamping, snorting horses.

But this particular offer came with some serious strings—attached, unfortunately, to a man she was finding extremely difficult to withstand.

She could feel her resistance to him slipping away every time she was with him and she knew she couldn't just surrender it without a fight. She couldn't afford to fall for a handsome charmer, not now when things were finally starting to go right.

"I don't think so." She put on her most brisk tone, the one she used with recalcitrant students throwing food in the lunch room. "Thank you for the offer, but we couldn't possibly intrude on a family event."

For a long moment he studied her, his head canted to one side, then he finally sighed. "I know you dislike me, Ms. Boyer—"

"I don't!" she protested instinctively.

"Come on. The kids can't hear us so you don't have to pretend for politeness' sake," he said. "I'm not sure how it happened or why but I always seem to rub you the wrong way. Whatever I did, can't we somehow figure out a way to move past it for one day, just so you can allow Cole and Morgan to participate in something we both know they'll enjoy?"

Oh! How could he make her so angry and so guilty at the same time? He was right, blast him. She wanted so much to say yes. Morgan, at least, would have a wonderful time. Cole would probably say it was all lame, but she had a feeling he would secretly enjoy it, too, especially with Seth around.

The only reason she resisted the invitation was because she wasn't so sure she could resist *him.*

How could she deprive her children of this opportunity to create a lasting memory because of her own weakness?

For two weeks she had been doing her best to keep him out of her head, to pretend cool indifference to him. She tried to convince herself the little hitch in her chest every time she drove onto the Cold Creek was simply a little heartburn from eating school lunch with her students.

She knew it wasn't. Even though he was as polite and friendly and noncharming as she could have asked for, her attraction to him only seemed to blossom.

Somehow—without apparently making any effort at all—Seth seemed to be whittling away at her defenses. The prospect of having to pretend disinterest for an entire day was daunting.

She could do it, she thought. For her children's sake, she could be tough, couldn't she?

"What time?" she finally said.

He grinned with triumph, looking so gorgeous in the thin, fading sunlight that she had to remind herself she was supposed to be resisting him.

"We're probably heading up right after morning chores, maybe around eleven or so. Does that work?"

"It should. Yes."

"Bring your father along if you'd like. He can ride a sled up or my mother and stepfather usually stay behind to hang out."

"All right. Thank you."

"Make sure you dress warmly. It's supposed to snow tonight so we'll have plenty of fresh powder."

She nodded as she slid into her car, wondering as she started the engine if the temperatures would possibly cool enough overnight to keep her unruly hormones in the deep freeze she'd stored them in for the last three years.

Chapter Five

She was a bright, successful woman who was certainly mature enough to know her own mind, Jenny thought the next morning as she drove along freshly plowed roads toward the Cold Creek.

So how had she let Seth Dalton con her into this? Through the long, snowy night, she'd had plenty of time to think through the ramifications of what she'd committed herself and her children to by agreeing to come on this outing today.

An entire day in his company. What had she been thinking?

Easy. Thinking apparently wasn't an activity she excelled at when Seth Dalton was around. The man only had to look at her and her brain cells decided to head to the Bahamas.

However this excursion had come about, she didn't doubt Cole and Morgan—and Jason, when it came to that—would enjoy the day. She had to keep that upper-most in her mind.

It was a beautiful morning, at least. Seth had been right about the snow. Maybe some ranching instinct helped him predict the weather—or maybe he just watched the forecast more assiduously than she did.

He had said they would have fresh snow today. As predicted, three to four inches had dropped on the area during the night, something she learned from her father wasn't at all unusual for mid- to late-November in eastern Idaho.

Everything was gorgeous: fresh and white and lovely. This was the perfect kind of early storm, just enough to cover the ground but not enough to make driving a nightmare.

Not much of one, anyway. Her SUV hit a wet spot suddenly and her wheels lost traction a little but she turned into the skid and quickly regained control.

"That's my girl." Jason smiled. "Watch your mother, Cole. Before much longer, you're going to be driving in these kind of conditions. You should be sure you pay attention now and follow her example."

"Does that mean I have to scream like a girl every time I hit a slick patch?" Cole asked with a smirk.

"Hey! I didn't scream," she exclaimed hotly. "That was simply a loud gasp."

Her father and son shared a conspiratorial look. She didn't mind being the source of their amusement, as long as Cole wasn't brooding in the backseat.

The rest of the drive passed smoothly and she wanted to think it was a good omen when the sun peeked through the clouds just as they reached the Cold Creek, gleaming off the snow that covered everything from fence lines to barns.

The Daltons' gravel drive had been cleared and sanded and she tried not to imagine Seth out here on a tractor taking care of his family's and his neighbors' driveways.

Why she found that such an appealing image, she couldn't begin to guess. Better to focus on the picture the ranch made as the pale sunlight glittered off the new snow.

She parked behind a silver pickup. Almost as if he'd been standing at the window watching for them, Seth hurried out of the house an instant later to greet them, accompanied by two puppies dancing around his feet.

He made a stunning picture, she had to admit, the strong, masculine figure in a Stetson and ranch coat, surrounded by playful puppies. Her insides gave a quick little shiver that had nothing to do with the weather, and she worried that even the presence of her father and children wouldn't be enough to insulate her from his effect on her.

She let out a breath. She was tough: she could do this. How hard could it be to resist the man for one day?

She received some inkling of the answer to that question when he reached to open the door, his broad, delighted smile somehow outshining the sun.

"You made it! I was afraid the snow might deter you."

She made some murmured reply—she wasn't quite sure what—and was relieved when he turned his attention to the rest of the vehicle's occupants. "Hey, Morgan. Cole. Mr. Chambers."

"Call me Jason," her traitor of a father said.

"Jason, then. Welcome to the Cold Creek. I'm so pleased you're all coming along with us today."

"Is that Lucy's brother?" Morgan asked, climbing out to greet the cavorting dogs.

"Sure is. This is Linus."

"They're so cute!" she exclaimed, giggling as they licked her.

"We're just about ready to go," Seth said. "I was just giving the sleds one more look. Jason, you are more than welcome to come up the mountain with us. Or if you'd prefer, my mom and stepfather and our neighbors, Viv and Guillermo Cruz, are staying behind to sit by the fire and enjoy a fierce game of gin rummy while the rest of us are slaving out in the cold hunting Christmas trees for them."

Jason perked up. "Now that sounds like my idea of fun."

"Come on inside, everyone, and I'll introduce you around."

"Are we going to ride horses to find our Christmas tree?" Morgan asked eagerly.

Seth reached down and tugged the long tail of her fleece stocking cap and something sharp and sweet yanked at Jenny's heart.

"Sorry, sweetheart, but it would take all day to get up to where the trees are on horseback. We usually go after our trees on snowmobiles. It's faster that way. But you and Natalie can maybe ride around the arena later when we come back down the mountain if you'd like."

So much for her Currier & Ives fantasy, Jenny thought wryly. A reality slap was just what she deserved for jumping to romantic conclusions. Noisy, growly snowmobiles didn't quite fit her idea of a perfect holiday, but she supposed they would be more efficient.

She shook her head at own foolishness but followed Seth and the two wrestling puppies up the cleared sidewalk into the large log-and-stone ranch house.

Inside, she was assaulted by warmth and welcome. A fire snapped in a huge river-rock fireplace and the house smelled of apples and cinnamon and the sharp scent of wood smoke. For all its size—the soaring ceilings and the grand wall of windows overlooking the western slope of the Tetons—the house struck her as comfortable instead of pretentious.

"We're just waiting for Jake and Maggie," Seth said. "They had some kind of emergency at the clinic but called a few minutes ago and said they were on their way. They shouldn't be long. Take your coats off out here and come in and meet everyone else."

She complied and spent a moment gathering everyone's coats then handing them to Seth. For a moment their arms brushed and she felt hard strength beneath the heavy fabric of his coat.

She had to hope nobody else—especially Seth—noticed she sucked in her breath at the contact.

Seth gave no indication that he had seen anything amiss as he took their coats and set them over the arm of a big plump armchair.

The kitchen was just as welcoming as the great room but on a smaller scale. Painted a cheery yellow, it was airy and bright, with crisp white appliances and a huge pine table overflowing with people.

She was assaulted by noise as everyone seemed to have something to say at once to welcome the newcomers.

The instant they walked in, Natalie—Morgan's good friend and daughter to Seth's oldest brother, Wade—jumped up from her chair with a squeal and ran to Morgan.

They hugged as if they'd been separated for months instead of merely overnight, before quickly running off.

Jason slid right into Natalie's newly vacant chair and immediately struck up a conversation with a distinguished-looking gentleman and a woman Jenny recognized as Marjorie Montgomery, Seth's mother.

That left her and Cole as the odd ones out. For an awkward moment she and her son stood on the fringe of the crowd, and she experienced a rare moment of sympathy for him.

She had always been a little hesitant about meeting new people, though she had been forced to work hard to overcome it through nearly fifteen years as an educator.

Cole was a great deal like her in that respect, she realized suddenly. Perhaps he feigned indifference— and sometimes even contempt—to hide his own social discomfort. It was an astonishing revelation.

"Have you met everyone?" Seth asked from behind her, his breath warm in her ear.

"No. Not really."

He quickly performed introductions to his mother and stepfather Quinn. Viviana and Guillermo Cruz both beamed at her in welcome. Seth introduced the man playing with the puppies Morgan had abandoned for her best friend as the best vet in town, Dave Summers, and his wife, Linda.

"My brother Wade is outside checking the snowmobiles and I told you Jake and Maggie are on their way. I'm not sure where Caroline is."

"Right here."

A voice spoke from behind her and Jenny turned and found Caroline Dalton walking into the kitchen, looking lovely and serene and extremely pregnant.

Jenny had met her at various school functions and knew she was married to Seth's oldest brother, Wade, and was stepmother to Wade's three children from a first marriage Marcy told her had ended with the tragic death of his wife just after the birth of their youngest child.

Caroline had always been friendly and kind, even when her stepson Tanner had been sent to Jenny's office for some mischief or other, and she had to admit she was grateful to see a familiar face.

"Cole, would you like a cookie?" she asked, and Jenny wanted to hug her for including him.

"Sure," he said, reaching for one.

He was just taking a big bite when they heard a commotion in the doorway. Jenny looked over to see a blond girl about Cole's age come into the kitchen holding hands with Tanner and Cody Dalton.

Cole hurried to swallow his cookie, straightening to his full height. He looked both surprised and pleased to see the girl.

"Uh, hey, Miranda," he said, his ears turning pink beneath his snowboarder toque.

She gave him a hesitant smile. "Hi, Cole," she said.

Jenny told herself she was glad her son had someone his own age to hang out with during this outing, though she wasn't sure she was ready to spend the day watching his painfully awkward adolescent interactions with a member of the opposite sex.

"This is Miranda Summers, Dave and Linda's daughter," Caroline said. "She's my lifesaver and watches the kids for me sometimes in the afternoon so I can get some work done."

Marcy—the eternally helpful fount of information that she was—had told her Caroline wrote motivational books and was also a very successful life coach.

Jenny wondered if Caroline Dalton might be able to offer any advice for a woman who seemed destined to be fascinated by the absolutely wrong sort of men.

"We were so thrilled when Seth said he had invited you and your family today," Caroline said with a warm smile that went a long way toward easing Jenny's worries about intruding.

"What a great idea and a wonderful chance for us to get to know you," Caroline went on. "I'm so glad you agreed to come."

"Your brother-in-law can be quite…" Annoying. Bossy. Manipulative. "…persuasive."

Caroline Dalton laughed. "That's an understatement."

"What can I say? It's a gift." Seth grinned, popping one of the cookies in his mouth. "I'm just full of them."

"You're certainly full of something," Caroline countered.

Seth only laughed and patted her abdomen with an easy familiarity that told Jenny they shared a close relationship.

"Don't listen to her, kid." He spoke in the general direction of Caroline's midsection. "A few more months and you can make up your own mind about who's your favorite uncle."

Caroline shook her head but with such affection Jenny wondered for an instant at their relationship.

Just then the outside door opened and Wade Dalton came into the increasingly crowded kitchen, stamping snow off his boots and hanging his Stetson on a hook by the door.

His gaze immediately went to his wife, and she smiled at him with such clear joy that Jenny felt foolish even wondering for an instant about Seth and Caroline.

The other woman was obviously crazy about her husband—and vice versa.

"What are we all waiting for here? The sleds are ready and the sun is shining. I say we get this done."

"Maggie and Jake aren't here yet," Caroline said. "They called a moment ago and said they were on their way."

"We can start suiting up anyway," he said. The veterinarian and his wife rose and started shrugging into heavy parkas.

She managed to wrench Cole's attention from Miranda long enough to drag him back to the ranch great room and their coats. For the next several minutes, they were all busy donning their winter gear—parkas, ski pants, thick gloves.

Jenny had just finished helping Morgan zip her coat when the front door opened, admitting two newcomers.

"You just made it," Seth said with a grin. "We were going to leave without you."

"I'm sure we would have survived the pain," his brother Jake said, his voice dry.

The woman with him—small, dark-haired and graceful as she maneuvered on forearm crutches—gave him a reproving look. "You can always stay here and play cards with the parents and I'll go up with the rest of them. I love cutting our own tree."

"We've got a nice Scotch pine in the backyard. Why couldn't we have saved ourselves the trouble and just cut that one so we could spend the day warm and dry by the fire?"

"Jenny, this complainer is my brother Jake and this beautiful creature is his wife, Maggie," Seth said, kissing the latter on the cheek. "This is Jennifer Boyer, the new principal at Pine Gulch Elementary."

She smiled. "I've met Dr. Dalton. Hello again. And nice to meet you," she added to Maggie, wondering about the crutches everyone else seemed to take in stride.

"Hi," Jake Dalton said. "And hello, Miss Morgan. How's the breathing today?"

"Good. Mom made me do a peak flow test before we left and it was ninety-five."

"Excellent!" He held out a hand for Morgan to high-five, which she did with a giggle.

Jenny had met Dr. Dalton soon after arriving in Pine Gulch when she had taken Morgan in for a refill of her asthma medication. Morgan had been to see him twice since then and each time, he struck Jenny as a very insightful, very compassionate physician, a combination that didn't always go together, in her experience.

"Maggie, sit down for a minute while you have the chance," he said to his wife.

"I'm fine," she said firmly.

"What's with the sticks?" Seth asked, a rude question, Jenny thought, but Maggie Dalton only made a face at him.

Before she could answer, the others came into the great room from the kitchen and Viviana Cruz caught sight of her daughter and hurried toward her.

The resemblance between them was startling, Jenny saw now they were together. The only significant difference was the hint of gray in Viviana's hair and some fine wrinkles in the corners of her eyes.

"Magdalena. What is this?" she asked, worry in her voice. "Why are you using the crutches today?"

"It is nothing, Mama. I promise. Just a little irritation, that's all. My personal physician insisted. I followed his advice since he tends to get pissy when I don't, but really, I'm fine."

"I don't get pissy," Jake growled. "I get even. Next time you put up a fuss, I'll just hide your prosthesis *and* your crutches and make you hop everywhere."

Jenny stared, stunned that the doctor she had come to respect so much would be so harsh with his wife. She was mortified when Maggie saw her shock and shook her head with a smile.

"He's teasing, Jenny, I promise. He wouldn't dare. I know all his hiding places anyway."

"What's a prosthesis?" Morgan asked, in one of those awkward moments all parents experience when they wish their children weren't so naturally curious.

Maggie Dalton didn't seem to mind. She pulled up her pant leg and Jenny saw her left leg ended just below her knee. "It's just a fancy word for a fake leg."

Morgan looked at the metal and plastic device with fascination. "Wow! Can you do cool stuff with it, like jump over cars and stuff?"

Maggie laughed. "Not yet, but I'm working on it."

Her mother still looked concerned. "If you are hurting, you should stay behind with us."

"No, Mama. I'm fine. I've been looking forward to this all week. I'll be sitting on the snowmobile the whole time, I promise."

Viviana bristled like she wanted to argue but her husband, a quiet, sturdy-looking man, put a hand on her arm and she subsided.

A short time later, everyone was ready and they walked outside in the cold air toward a row of gleaming machines.

Jenny gulped. Was she expected to drive one of these complicated-looking beasts? She knew absolutely nothing about snowmobiles. She wouldn't have the first idea how to even start the thing, forget about taking it up a mountain.

To her relief, Seth turned to Cole as soon as they reached the snowmobiles. "Cole, if I take your sister behind me, do you think you can handle driving one with your mom?"

A silly question to ask a fourteen-year-old obsessed with machines. His eyes lit up brighter than Jenny had seen in a long time.

"Oh, yeah," he said with a grin.

"Is it legal?" she asked warily.

"Absolutely or I wouldn't have suggested it," he assured her. "Let's show you how it works."

For the next few moments, he walked Cole through the steps for operating the snowmobile and even had him drive it twenty yards or so before coming back.

"You're all set," Seth assured him.

"Get on, Mom," Cole said gleefully.

She sent Seth a hesitant look but he gave her a reassuring smile. "He'll be great, I promise. I'll keep an eye on you the whole time."

She climbed on, grabbing tight, and realized everyone else was mounted and ready—even Morgan waited on the back of Seth's snowmobile for her driver.

Seth took a few more moments to give Cole some final instructions and she found herself impressed by both his patience and by his consideration. "We'll be climbing into the mountains but it's all pretty gentle and easy. I'll be right ahead of you and will keep an eye on you, and Dave and Linda will bring up the rear."

He paused and gave Cole a stern look. "No hotdogging, okay? Not with your mom on board."

Cole grimaced but nodded. Seth grinned at them both, then climbed onto his own sled and headed off after the others.

"You ready, Mom?" Cole asked.

She grabbed him tightly around his waist, wondering if Seth had arranged things this way so she could remember the joy and connection of being a team with her son.

"Let's go," she said.

With a little jerk, Cole pulled the snowmobile forward and they were off, following Morgan and Seth up the mountain.

Chapter Six

Seth pulled his snowmobile to a stop and turned around to watch Cole and Jenny's progress up the track through virgin snow Wade had cut with his bigger sled.

"Why are we stopping?" Morgan asked behind him, her voice pitched loud to be heard over the growling engines.

"Just checking on the slowpokes," he told her.

She laughed and lifted her face up to the sunshine. Morgan was a sweet kid, he thought, so appreciative of everything. She treated a simple snowmobile ride into the mountains like it was the grandest adventure of her young life.

He was a little surprised at how much he was enjoying this. When he was trying to figure out sled assignments earlier in the morning, he had instinctively wanted Jenny to ride with him. He was more than ready to ramp things up a level, to make her unable to avoid confronting the physical connection he sensed between them.

What better way than to have her holding tightly to him up and down the mountain? He had spent more than a few pleasant moments fantasizing about having her so close to him for the entire half-hour ride up and back down again.

On further reflection, he'd discarded the idea, appealing as it was. Crowding her physically would only push her away. This arrangement was better.

It was not only more safe to have Morgan with him rather than her inexperienced brother but it also provided the bonus of being able to watch Jenny enjoying a fun, peaceful moment with her son, something he'd figured out early wasn't a frequent occurrence between the two.

He hadn't expected to get such a kick out of Jenny's daughter, but he was discovering he enjoyed having her look at him as though he was some kind of hero.

In talking over the Christmas-tree excursion with Wade, they had decided to sandwich experienced drivers around the teens. Wade and his boy Tanner were riding point with Miranda driving a sled and Natalie riding behind her.

Dave and Linda were just ahead of Seth and Morgan, to keep an eye on the girls. Cole and Jenny were behind him, with Maggie and Jake bringing up the rear on another of the bigger snowmobiles. They also towed the sled that would be used to haul down the Christmas trees.

So far the arrangement seemed to be working. He couldn't remember the last time he'd enjoyed himself so much on the annual Dalton Christmas-Tree Trek. A big part of that came from the vicarious enjoyment he found watching Jenny and her kids.

"Are we almost there?" Morgan asked.

"Not much farther. See that small valley of pines up

there about halfway up the mountain? That's where we're headed. It should take us about fifteen more minutes. How are the lungs up this high?"

She took a deep, noisy breath. "Great," she assured him.

He was going to tell her to make sure she let him know if she started having any trouble with her asthma, but just then Cole pulled up alongside him.

"What's the matter?" he called over the noise of the sleds.

"Just checking on you. Everything going okay?"

He nodded. "This is a kick!"

"Jenny? How about you?"

She smiled at him, her cheeks wind-chapped and her color high. She looked so bright and vibrant out in the cold sunshine that he had to fight a fierce desire to tug her off the sled and into his arms.

"It's wonderful! The view from up here is absolutely incredible!"

"It is," he agreed, though he was hard-pressed to drag his gaze away from her excitement.

With effort, he managed to do it and turn back to her son. "Cole, I wanted to show you where to go from here. We're heading for that stand of trees about halfway up there."

"Okay," the boy said. "Though I'm pretty sure I'm capable of following a trail made by four other snow-mobiles."

"I'm sure you are, but sometimes it helps to have the bigger picture about where you're ultimately heading, instead of just following the exhaust of the machine in front of you."

"If I was stupid enough to veer off the trail, you'd all be on me like stink on cheese anyway."

He laughed. "Just so you know where you stand, kid."

Cole made a face at him. "Are we going to ride or are we going to sit around shooting the breeze all day?"

Jake and Maggie pulled up before he could answer. He gave his sister-in-law a careful look but she didn't look to be in terrible pain, even though she had her crutches handy.

He knew Jake would never have let her come along if he worried she might overdo it, so Seth decided he would let his brother worry about his own wife.

"You're blocking the trail," Jake called.

"Yeah, yeah. We're going."

He started his sled again, feeling a curious warmth in his chest when Morgan gripped him tightly.

If he wasn't careful, he could seriously fall for Jenny Boyer's kids, he thought. That would be great if their mother came with them in a package deal but he was afraid things wouldn't work out that way.

This was a stupid idea.

An hour later, Seth wondered how in Hades he was going to make it through an entire day pretending this casual friendship with Jenny when he hungered for far more, especially since she seemed determined to push him away at every turn.

The more time he spent with her, the deeper his fascination for her seemed to run. It baffled and unnerved him. He didn't understand it—he just knew he couldn't seem to keep his eyes off her.

He was blowing all his plans to be cool and detached and to give her the time and space she needed until she was ready for him to kick things up a notch. Things weren't working out that way, mainly because he couldn't force himself to stay away from her.

Though he knew he should have let one of his brothers help her while he cut the trees for his mother and the Cruzes, he still found himself trailing after Jenny and her kids, his chainsaw at the ready as they scoured the stand of evergreens for the perfect tree.

What he really wanted to do was drag her behind the closest trunk and steal any chance to explore that mouth, just so he could see if it could possibly taste as delicious as it looked.

With her two kids along, the possibility of that was fairly remote, he acknowledged. Still, a man could dream.

"This is way more fun than pulling our artificial tree out of storage like we've always done," a pink-cheeked Morgan exclaimed as they trudged through the snow toward the outer edge of the small forest.

He locked away his inappropriate lust and put on an exaggerated expression of horror. "Artificial. Please say it's not so."

Morgan giggled. "Yep."

"Don't tell me it's pink."

Jenny made a face at him. "Of course not. It was a perfectly lovely seven-and-a-half-foot spruce. Green, prelit and very convenient."

"That smells like the petroleum product that it is, no doubt. How can you stand here inhaling this delicious scent into your lungs and even consider having an artificial tree?"

"We gave it to Goodwill when we moved. And we're here now, aren't we, searching for the perfect tree? That has to count for something!"

"I don't know. Somebody who's always had an artificial monstrosity might not recognize the perfect tree even if it reached out a branch and tapped you on the head with it."

She stopped suddenly, so abruptly he almost plowed into her. Her gaze was glued to a blue spruce about eight feet high. Though a yellow ribbon tied to the trunk indicated he'd marked it for thinning, now he couldn't really see anything spectacular about it.

Jenny apparently did. She gave a happy sigh. "This one. I want this one."

He wasn't ready for the search to be over yet. Then they would have to go back and rejoin the rest of his family and he would lose any chance for privacy with her.

"There are still maybe a half dozen marked ones we haven't even looked at yet. Are you sure this is the one?"

"Positive. This one is perfect, don't you guys think?"

Morgan nodded with the same kind of glee as her mother but Cole only shrugged. "It looks like every other tree we've seen today," he said.

"What are you talking about?" Jenny exclaimed. "This tree has personality! It's wonderful! The color is a far richer green than all the rest and can't you see the way all the branches look so perfect except for that little one there in the back pointing in a different direction?"

"If you say so."

"It's just right. I only wish the school didn't have a fire-code policy against real trees or I'd put it out by the office."

She looked so thrilled, so bubbly and excited, Seth couldn't look away. Her eyes glowed and her nose was red and he couldn't seem to think about anything but tasting that bright smile.

He cleared his throat and made himself focus on the tree instead. "You want it, it's yours. Cole, you want to do the honors?"

The kid eyed the big machine in his hands with unmistakable longing, then he looked away. "You can do it."

He probably didn't know the first thing about running a chainsaw, Seth realized. "It's easy. Come on. I'll walk you through it."

He showed Cole how to fire up the saw, then helped guide him to the right spot on the trunk. Between the two of them, they buzzed through the small trunk in seconds and the tree fell in a flurry of snow. It was a good choice, he thought, one of those he'd marked that were being crowded out by bigger trees.

"How are we going to carry our tree down the mountain now?" Morgan asked.

"Jake is pulling a sled behind his snowmobile. We'll tie them all together on that and he and Maggie will drag them down."

"Is that it?" Cole asked.

"I've got to cut one for my place now. Since you're so good at picking them out, you can help me find mine. With my vaulted ceilings, I've got room for a ten- or twelve-foot one. Think big."

They spent several moments walking through the heavy timber looking at possibilities until Jenny stopped in front of the one he'd actually had in mind for his place all along.

"Kids, your mother is a natural at Christmas-tree hunting. Just think what she must have been suppressing through all those years of artificial trees!"

Again he urged Cole to do the honors, though this time he let the boy handle the saw by himself, keeping a careful watch on him as he did.

"Why don't you to go back to the one we cut for your house and carry it down to the snowmobiles while your mom helps me haul this one?" he suggested. "Can you find the way?"

"We can see it from here." Cole pointed down the hill to the sleds gleaming in the pale sunshine. He took off with Morgan following close behind, and finally Seth was alone with Jenny, just as he'd orchestrated.

He hadn't expected her to be looking at him with such a warm smile. "Thank you for this," she said. "You were right, it will be a wonderful memory for Cole and Morgan."

"What about for you?"

Her gaze flashed for just an instant then she looked away. He saw her swallow and would have given half his horses—and a cow or two, as well—to know what she was thinking.

"I've enjoyed it," she murmured.

"You don't relax enough. You should do it more often."

Her mouth opened, her expression indignant. Instead of the sharp retort he expected, after a moment she closed her mouth and sighed. "You're right. I know you're right but it's not always the easiest thing in the world for me to do with any success."

He dared take a step closer, keeping his hands carefully neutral at his sides. "Why is that, I wonder?"

Her gaze flitted back to his and stayed there a little longer, like a wild bird following a trail of sunflower seeds toward an outstretched hand. "I suppose because so much depends on me. It's hard work being a principal and even harder work being a single mother."

"You do both very well."

"And how would you know that? You don't have children in my school to judge my performance there and you don't have children of your own at home to comment on my mothering."

"You don't have to be a jockey to recognize a great racehorse."

She gave a short laugh. "I don't believe I've ever been compared to a horse before."

He debated backing off now, giving her a chance to regroup, then decided that would be foolish. Better to keep her off balance. He stepped forward again until only a foot or so separated them. From here, he could smell the fresh, flowery scent of her, an unlikely beacon of spring amid the wintry landscape.

She swallowed hard at his nearness but didn't step back. Instead, her chin lifted. "I don't like to be crowded, Seth."

For some strange reason, her defiance made him laugh. "Is that what I was doing?"

"Oh, I have no doubt you know exactly what you're doing. You're very good at what you do. I certainly won't deny that."

"What I do?"

"The whole seduction bit. The oh-so-casual touches, those sexy, intimate smiles. Stepping closer and closer until I can't focus on anything but you. I imagine most women probably melt in a big puddle at your feet."

The cynicism in her voice smarted. "But not you?"

"I'm sorry if that stings your pride but I'm just not interested. I believe I told you that."

"So you did," he agreed. "But are you so sure about that, Ms. Boyer?"

Against the howl of all his instincts, he stepped closer again. He watched a tiny pulse jump in her throat and her breathing seemed to accelerate. The hunger inside him to taste her threatened to consume him, to wipe out whatever remained of his self-control and his sanity.

"Ye-es," she said, though that single word came out breathy, hushed.

"I think we both know that's not precisely true," he murmured. He reached out and gripped the ends of her scarf in some halfhearted effort to keep her from fleeing, then leaned down slowly, carefully, anticipation thrumming powerfully inside him.

An instant before his mouth would have at last found hers, some subconscious warning system picked up rustling in the underbrush. He dropped her scarf and stepped back just before Wade walked into their little clearing.

His brother surveyed the scene, his hard blue eyes missing nothing, but he only sent one swift, censorious look in Seth's direction. "Cole and Morgan said you cut a big one for your place. I came to see if you need help hauling it down so we can go back down the mountain. My boys are starting to get restless and I think Cody's ready for a nap."

"Yeah. We're on our way."

What the hell was he doing? Seth wondered as he and Wade hauled the big tree down the slope toward the waiting sleds. He had played that last hand like some damn greenhorn who'd never kissed a girl before. That's what was called jumping the gate before the starting pistol sounded.

She wanted him to back off. Hell, she'd practically *ordered* him to, and he'd ignored her. He had no doubt he would have had her pressed up against one of those trees in another ten seconds if Wade hadn't interrupted.

He didn't like the fact that he'd almost lost it back there, that he'd plunged ahead with something that all his instincts were telling him was a bad idea. It wasn't like him at all. He always, *always,* maintained some control over himself when it came to women.

Jenny Boyer somehow managed to shred that control to bits, like a chainsaw ripping through flimsy cardboard.

Where did he go from here? He didn't want to give up before he'd even enjoyed a tiny taste of that lush mouth, but he might just have to accept the grim reality that some things weren't meant to be.

She wanted him to leave her alone. Maybe that was what he ought to do. Forget about Jennifer Boyer, just as she had insisted, and move on. The thought filled him with an odd kind of restlessness but he didn't see any other choice. If she wasn't interested—or didn't *want* to be interested—he had to respect her boundaries.

He was subdued on the ride back down the mountain and everyone else seemed to be, too. A light snow started falling again and while it looked feathery and lovely when you were safe and dry inside watching it through the window, on a snowmobile, it pelted exposed skin like sharp pebbles. Everyone seemed glad when they reached the Cold Creek again.

At the house, they quickly unloaded the trees from the transport sled. Maggie was looking tired and the kids were cold, so Jake and Wade sent the women and children inside the ranch house to warm up.

While they tied the trees onto the respective vehicles for transport to their destination, Seth drove the Cold Creek snowmobiles into the storage garage and performed postride maintenance checks on them. He was the default mechanic on the ranch, and he liked to think he was the go-to guy when machines broke down.

He had just stowed the last one and was checking fluid levels on it when Jake showed up in the doorway of the garage.

"I'm about done here," Seth said. "Go ahead inside and check on Maggie."

"She'll be okay."

"What's her deal today, anyway? I haven't seen her use the canes for a long time. She said she was having some irritation. Is everything okay?"

"She's changing pain meds and we're trying to find a good safe combination."

His brother gave him a quiet smile that told wonders about how much he adored his wife. "Don't tell anybody, but we're talking about starting a family and Maggie wants to wean off some of her heavy-duty meds before we give it a serious try."

He felt another of those curious pangs in his chest. Both of his brothers were deliriously happy with their wives and their lives. He was glad for them, he told himself. He just couldn't quite figure out why the life he had always thought was perfect suddenly felt so empty in comparison.

"That's wonderful," he said. "I can't think of two people who would make better parents."

When Jake continued to stand in the doorway watching him, Seth sighed, screwed the oil cap back on the snowmobile and stood up to wait for the lecture he sensed was coming.

He knew that look in his brother's eyes all too well. Wade must have seen more of that encounter with Jenny on the mountain than he thought and sent Jake in to do his dirty work.

"Let's have it, then," he said.

"What?"

"You've got on your bossy-big-brother look. Wade was the one giving me the snake eye all the way down the mountain so how did you get to be the one roped into this?"

Jake leaned against the door frame. "We drew straws and I lost."

"Lucky you."

"Right. That means I get to be the one to ask you what the hell you think you're doing."

He really wasn't in the mood for this, Seth decided. He'd been on the receiving end of these little improving talks all his life from one or both of his brothers. He had to wonder if Wade and Jake would still feel inclined to tell him how to live his life when he was seventy.

Probably.

"I believe I'm putting the sleds away right now. You or Wade have a problem with that?"

"You know we don't. Do what you want with the snowmobiles. But neither of us is too crazy about you tangling up a nice lady like Principal Boyer."

He arched an eyebrow. "Tangling up?"

"You know what I mean. What are you doing here, Seth? She's not your usual bar babe. She's a nice woman with a couple of kids and a retired father and a responsible job. She deserves better."

His brothers sure knew just how to twist the knife in his gut. "Thanks," he snapped. "It's always nice to get a vote of support from my family. Don't hold back, doc. Why don't you tell me what a selfish, irresponsible bastard I am, so we can all go in and have some lunch?"

Jake had always been slow to anger but he also never backed down from a fight. "Oh, screw the poor-me routine. That wasn't what I meant and you know it. I'm not talking about you as a person, I'm referring strictly to your usual playbook with women."

Seth yanked down the seat of the sled so hard he was pretty sure he broke something. "Memorized it, have you?"

"Since you've been sticking to the same game plan since before you were old enough to shave, it's not tough to guess where this is headed."

"And where is that?"

"You wine her, dine her, romance her, take what you want, then move on to the next lovely young thing to cross your path."

"Yeah, yeah. Selfish, irresponsible bastard. I got that part."

"I didn't say that. Most of the time the women you hook up with know what to expect and probably are only after exactly what you're willing to give them. Fine. If you're both consenting adults, no harm no foul. But this is different. Jennifer Boyer isn't one of your Bandito bimbos. She's got kids, Seth, one of them a teenager who looks up to you. From what I hear, Cole has already been abandoned by his father. Don't you think you're only going to reinforce that lousy example of how a man should treat a woman when he watches you walk away from his mother, too?"

"I haven't even kissed the woman!"

"But you want to, don't you?"

"None of your business."

"It's not," Jake agreed. "But I have to point out those kids already care about you and if you take things where I think you want to, Cole and Morgan are likely to come out of this mighty damn hurt when you get bored and move on."

He hadn't given much thought to their feelings in all this, he realized, with no small amount of shame.

"There's a whole forest full of pretty young trees out there," Jake went on. "Find a different one to scratch your itch on. That's all I'm saying."

"What if I don't want a different one?"

He hadn't meant to say that, but somehow the words slipped out anyway. Jake gave him a long, hard look that made him feel like he was fifteen years old again.

"Maybe for once you ought to try thinking not so

much about what *you* want but about what *she* wants, and see how that works out for you."

Before he could come up with some undoubtedly pithy reply, Jake left in that frustrating way of his.

Seth should have been relieved the lecture was over but he couldn't stop thinking about what his brother said. The hell of it was, he was absolutely right.

Jenny wanted nothing to do with him. Though he knew she was attracted to him despite her protests, he wasn't going to crowd her anymore, he decided.

He would still have to see her because of his arrangement with Cole. But after today, he would just be polite and friendly and forget about anything else.

No matter how impossible it suddenly seemed.

Chapter Seven

She was going to have a tough time dragging everyone away.

Jenny surveyed her family crowded around the Daltons' big kitchen and tried to remember the last time she'd seen them all enjoying a meal so much. Yes, the food was fabulous—a half-dozen different kinds of soup, hot rolls and a salad bar that rivaled anything in a restaurant— but the company was the most appealing part of this meal.

Morgan and Natalie were giggling at the smaller table brought in for the children. At the breakfast bar, Cole and Miranda were deep in a debate over the best ska band of all time. Even Jason was in his element laughing at something Quinn Montgomery said, down at the other end of the big dining table.

It was noisy and crowded and warm but her family seemed to be thriving. In fact, everyone seemed to be having a wonderful time except for her.

She couldn't seem to relax and allow herself to have fun. The Daltons had been everything kind. She found them all warm and friendly—even Seth's oldest brother, Wade. At first he had seemed gruff and intimidating, but throughout the day he had treated her and the children with nothing but kindness.

Despite the jovial company, she couldn't seem to move past her own awkward discomfort.

She was also painfully aware that everyone at the big table had been divided by couple—so by default she sat next to Seth. She had a hard time focusing on anything else but his nearness throughout the meal, his strong hands and his seductive masculine scent and the heat that seemed to shimmer off him in waves.

She didn't want to be here. She would have preferred sitting at the children's table to enduring this close proximity, especially as Seth had been distant and distracted throughout the meal and seemed to become more so as the meal wore on.

He obviously had second thoughts about inviting her and her family and regretted their de facto pairing.

Despite the fabulous food, her stomach felt hollow and achy and she wanted to disappear. That, in turn, made her angry with herself and more determined to see this dinner through as quickly as possible. At least they were already having dessert so the torture would be over soon.

"This pie is delicious," Caroline Dalton exclaimed from across the table with her warm smile. "I love the crunchy caramel topping."

Jenny smiled politely as others at the table joined in the praise for the caramel apple pie she'd brought along, one of her very few specialties. But even as she smiled and thanked them all for the compliments, she was aware of Seth next to her setting down his fork as if he were suddenly eating fried motor oil, leaving the rest of his pie uneaten on his plate.

A few moments later, he pushed back his chair and aimed his charming smile around the table at every single person but her.

"Thanks for a delicious meal, everybody, but I've got to run up to the barn."

"Can we go, Uncle Seth?" Natalie asked. "You said maybe we could ride later."

"You could go for a horseback ride, I guess." He paused then looked as if he regretted his words even as he spoke them. "Or Cole could grab one of the snowmobiles and pull you up the hill behind the barn so you can tube down. If it's all right with your mother, of course."

Natalie, Morgan and Tanner looked ecstatic at the possibility and even Cole and Miranda appeared thrilled.

"Oh, please, Mom!" Morgan begged.

How was she supposed to refuse with all those young eyes looking at her with identical entreaties?

"Thanks," she murmured under her breath to Seth.

He gave a smile that seemed only slightly repentant—but at least he wasn't completely ignoring her the way he'd done since that breathless moment on the mountain when he'd nearly kissed her.

"I suppose, if it's all right with the other parents."

"You all just warmed up," Caroline exclaimed. "Are you sure you want to go back out in the cold?"

The children gave a resounding answer in the affirmative and scrambled up from the chairs to climb back into their cold-weather gear.

Half an hour later, they were being pulled up the hill in turns by Cole on the snowmobile, who appeared to be having the time of his life.

Caroline had volunteered to go with them to keep an

eye on the children while the others stayed behind to watch a holiday movie. Though Jenny hadn't wanted to spend another minute with Seth, she had also hated thinking of the pregnant woman standing out in the snow.

"I'll do it," she insisted, so here she sat on a bench overlooking the sledding hill.

At least she didn't have to endure more stilted conversation with Seth. After dragging her into this whole thing, he had been astonishingly quick to disappear.

The minute Cole had the snowmobile tow rope figured out, Seth spent a few moments starting a small fire in a small cast-iron outdoor fireplace nearby, then claimed he had some things to do inside the horse barn that couldn't wait.

She hadn't minded sitting alone watching the children. It gave her a chance again to savor the magnificence of the setting. She found a raw grandeur in the snow-covered landscape with the backdrop of wild, rugged mountains.

Though sunset was still a few hours away, the afternoon sky was already beginning to turn lavender and it had started snowing again, big, fluffy flakes that made her want to catch one on her tongue like the children on her playground.

After a moment, she gave into the temptation and stuck out her tongue. Of course, it was at that instant that Seth walked out of the barn, apparently finished with what had been so urgent.

She jerked her tongue back into her mouth and kept it firmly planted there as he stood at the open doorway watching her. She had to hope he hadn't seen that completely childish impulse, though she had a feeling it was a vain hope.

After a moment he pulled the door closed behind him

and approached her, looking solid and dark and almost predatory against the snowy white landscape.

She hated herself for the little flutter in her stomach but couldn't seem to control it.

He sat down beside her on the bench. "Looks like they're having a good time. This was always the perfect sledding hill when we were kids."

She couldn't quite manage to wrap her mind around the image of this wholly masculine man in front of her as a gleeful child sledding down the hillside.

"This is much more fun with deeper snow," he went on. "You'll have to bring Morgan and Cole back in a month or so when the conditions are a little better."

The chances of that were fairly slim, she thought. "I can't believe we're still a week away from Thanksgiving and your mountains have more than two feet of snow."

"Better get used to it. We probably won't see bare earth again until March or April at the earliest. The higher elevations might be two or three months after that."

She shuddered, earning a laugh from him. "Didn't your dad warn you about our winters before you moved down from Seattle?"

"He told me they were on the harsh side but he's promised me the summers make up for it."

He smiled a little, though she thought he was still distant. "That's true enough. My mother always says if you complain about the winter, you don't deserve the summer."

"I guess I should watch my mouth, then."

"Just find a winter sport you enjoy, like ice climbing or cross-country skiing. That tends to give you a completely different perspective on the cold weather."

The idea of that wasn't very appealing, since she

figured she was probably about the most unathletic person in town. "Does curling up by the woodstove with a good book count?" she asked.

He grinned. "Sure. And you get bonus points if it's at least a book about winter sports."

"I'll have to dig through Dad's library to see what I can find about hockey or ice fishing," she said with a laugh. "I'm all for coming up with anything to make the winter pass more quickly."

"If you're not much of a cold-weather lover, what brings you to Pine Gulch?" he asked. "I would think a school principal could find work just about anywhere."

"Maybe. But I couldn't find my dad anywhere but here. He loves Pine Gulch. After the divorce, he offered to come live with us in Seattle but I knew he would hate it there. All the friends he made after he retired are here and he's got a rich, fulfilling life. The fishing, the photography, his monthly poker game with his friends in Jackson. I couldn't drag him away from that."

Jenny paused, surprised by her compulsion to confide in him. She wouldn't have thought it possible but Seth could actually be a comfortable conversationalist, if she could put her hormones on hold.

"At the same time, I knew my children needed him. Especially Cole. A boy his age needs strong male role models. Since his father's not in the picture anymore, I had to do something. When the principal position opened up at the elementary school, it seemed like an opportunity I couldn't pass up."

Their situation wasn't perfect, but she couldn't regret moving here. She was trying to do the best she could.

"So that's why you took the job at the elementary school and moved to town?" he asked. "To be near your dad?"

"I had to do something. Cole was in trouble almost all the time in Seattle. I hoped moving him here would steady him a little. Of course, six weeks later, he managed to steal and wreck a classic car," she said wryly.

"He's doing a good job of making it right, though."

"You know, the first month or so after we moved here, I thought I'd made a terrible mistake. These last few weeks have been much better. Whatever you've been doing with Cole, thank you."

Seth raised an eyebrow at her words and she saw surprise flicker in the deep blue of his eyes. "I haven't done anything but put him to work," he answered.

"Maybe that's exactly what he needed. A project to focus on. Or perhaps simply someone taking an interest in him. I don't know what it is, I only know things have improved considerably since he started coming out here. He doesn't seem to hate either me or Idaho as much as he used to."

"I'm glad," he said simply.

They sat in silence for a moment, broken only by the distant shrieks of the children and the snap of the fire in the little stove.

This was nice, she thought. Too nice. She could feel herself slipping under his spell again—and this time she couldn't really blame the man, since he wasn't doing anything but sitting there.

She was relieved when Cole pulled up to them a few moments later, breaking the fragile mood.

"Your turn, Mom," her son said. "Hop on. You can use Morgan's inner tube."

Jenny shook her head vigorously. "No. That's okay. I like my legs unbroken, thanks."

Astride the snowmobile, Cole flapped his arms and made a clucking sound. "Come on. Morgan's gone down six or seven times and she's only nine. Is she tougher than you?"

"Oh, without question."

"Come on," Cole cajoled. "Everybody's having a great time. You can't sit down here the whole time."

"You'll have fun," Seth joined in. "You can count this as your first experiment in winter sports."

She gazed at the two males, so physically dissimilar but so surprisingly alike, then sighed and rose from the bench.

"I'm blaming you when this goes horribly wrong," she told Seth with a laugh as she climbed onto the snowmobile behind her son.

Her smile faded when she realized Seth was staring at her mouth. Awareness bloomed in her stomach and she was almost grateful when Cole gunned the engine and started up the mountainside.

He needed to get out of there.

Fast.

All his lofty intentions were being shot straight to hell the more time he spent with Jenny Boyer.

He watched her on the snowmobile behind her son as the boy climbed to the top of the hill.

Even from here, he could see the tension in her posture. She clearly didn't want to be up there but she was doing it anyway, refusing to let her fears hold her back. He admired that in a woman.

He admired a lot about her. He liked the way her eyes lit up when she talked about her children, he liked the way she seemed to sincerely listen to a person, he liked the way she was willing to laugh at herself.

He let out a heavy breath. What the hell good did it do to count down all the things he liked about her? The grim fact remained that Jake was absolutely right. She deserved somebody better than him, somebody who wasn't always looking around the next bend.

He'd been crazy to come out here again. He should have just holed up in the barn until she was gone, taking her big green eyes and her lush mouth and her sweet-as-sugar smile with her.

From here, he could see her arguing with her children, then a minute later she climbed onto the inner tube. She sat there for a long moment, then nodded to her kids, who gave her a push.

She shrieked then he heard her exclamation turn into a delighted laugh that seemed to reach right through him and tug at his insides.

He should make his escape while he had the chance, he thought. He even turned around and headed for the barn but he'd only made three steps when he heard the laughter cut off into an abrupt scream.

He jerked back around just in time to watch her spiral off the inner tube. The tube went one way and she went the other. To his horror she rolled three, possibly four times, then she lay horribly still about twenty yards from the bottom.

He was already racing up the slope before she came to a stop, his heart pumping like crazy. He reached her just seconds later, astonished by his protective impulses. He wanted to grab her close and hang on tight.

"Jen. Talk to me, sweetheart."

She didn't answer, though he could see her chest rising and falling beneath her winter parka. He unzipped it just as Cole roared up on the snowmobile.

"Go down to the ranch house and get my brother Jake," he told the boy, whose face was as white as the landscape around them. "Hurry."

"Right. Okay."

He gunned the snowmobile and took off down the road and Seth turned his attention back to Jenny.

His brother might be the doctor in the family but years of ranch living and dealing with various mishaps had given Seth a basic knowledge of first aid. He ran his hands over her but couldn't find any broken bones.

By now Miranda, Tanner and the girls had gathered, watching him solemnly as he examined her. Tanner and the younger girls looked terrified and even the normally sensible Miranda seemed anxious.

The snow had kicked up in the last few moments and giant flakes drifted down to settle on her still features, alighting on her eyelashes, in her hair, on the curves of her cheek.

By his estimation, it would take Cole ten minutes or so to ride down to the house, grab Jake and drive back up here. He couldn't bear the idea of Jenny lying out here in the snow all that time.

Besides that, the children needed to be inside where they could get warm. All of them were going to be shocky soon if they didn't go inside.

Making a split-second decision, he scooped Jenny into his arms. Moving her some place warm and dry out-weighed the first aid axiom about not moving her, he decided. Jake would probably yell at him, but he knew his brother would have done the same.

"Miranda, I'm taking Ms. Boyer inside. Come with me and take the kids into the kitchen, okay? I've got some cookies and I think there's some hot cocoa mix somewhere in there. Morgan, Nat, I need you two to help Miranda with Tanner."

"What about my mom?" Morgan asked. Her features were pale with fright. He could only hope she didn't have an asthma attack just now since he wasn't sure he could cope with a second crisis.

He gave her what he hoped was a reassuring smile as he carried Jenny into his house. "She just bumped her head a little when she fell off the inner tube but I'm sure everything's going to be fine. Aren't we lucky to have a doctor so close? Jake will take care of her, I promise."

"Why are her eyes still closed?" she asked as he set her mother down carefully on the coach.

He'd been the one pushing her to go on that tube, he thought with guilt. "Have you ever fallen at the playground and had the wind knocked out of you? That's what happened to your mom."

He took time away from his worry over Jenny to give Morgan a quick, reassuring hug. She seemed to find comfort from it—and so did he. "Go on into the kitchen with the others and as soon as Dr. Jake takes a look at her, you can come back and talk to her, okay?"

"She always stays with me and holds my hand when I'm having a flare-up. Will you stay with her?"

"I'm not going anywhere, honey," he promised.

With one last anxious look, she went into the kitchen and he turned his attention back to Jenny.

She looked so frail against the dark maroon leather of his couch. A moment ago she had been laughing with him and complaining about the weather and now she was so terribly still.

He pulled her coat open and was running a hand over her again, looking more carefully this time for anything out of the ordinary when her eyes fluttered open.

She gazed at him for a long moment, her eyes hazy and baffled, then she blinked and seemed to become more alert by the second.

"Seems like a lot of trouble to go to just so you could cop a cheap feel," she mumbled, her voice hoarse.

Relief flooded through him and he closed his eyes for a moment and said a silent prayer of gratitude. She couldn't be at death's door if she could manage a tart comment like that.

He grinned, fighting the urge to pull her into his arms. "That was just a side benefit. And believe me, it wasn't cheap in the least."

To his surprise, she smiled back, then winced at the movement.

"What hurts, besides your head?"

"What doesn't?" She tried to pull herself to a sitting position.

He shook his head. "Take it easy. I'm not letting you go anywhere so you might as well relax for now."

She obeyed, though he thought her compliance stemmed more from her lack of strength than any-thing else.

"Nothing seems broken from what I could tell," he told her. "Any acute areas of pain?"

"Only my head. Most of me is just one big ache except my head, which I'm afraid might be ready to fall off."

"It wouldn't surprise me if you've got a concussion. You conked it pretty hard."

She winced. "Graceful, as usual."

Tenderness washed through him and he couldn't prevent himself from picking up her hand. Strictly to warm her cold fingers, he told himself, even as he savored the contact. "It was just your trajectory. You couldn't avoid that rock, no matter what you tried to do. Anybody would have crashed in the same situation."

"Thank you for trying to make me feel better," she murmured.

Her fingers curled in his and a terrifying tenderness seemed to soak through him. "Is it working?"

She made a face. "Not really."

They both shared a small laugh he found oddly intimate and again he had to fight the fierce desire to pull her into his arms.

"Where are my kids?" she asked.

"Morgan's in the kitchen with Miranda and the others and I sent Cole down to the house on the snowmobile for Jake. They should be here in a minute. Matter of fact, if I'm not mistaken, I hear an engine out there right now."

Seth barely had time to pull his hand away from hers before Jake and Cole both burst into the house.

Chapter Eight

"I'm sorry about this," Jenny said five minutes later to Jake Dalton as he gave her a careful exam after banishing Seth and Cole from the room. "I feel like such an idiot."

He smiled with the calm competence she'd noticed during Morgan's asthma-related office visits. "Don't worry about it. You're not the first one to ever tumble down that hill. I think all of us have done our share. Seth even broke his collarbone on that hill when he was around Morgan's age. I don't suppose he told you that, did he?"

"No. He didn't mention it."

"He saw some snowboarders on TV and thought he'd like to try it."

"Oh, no," she murmured.

"Exactly. We didn't have any equipment, of course, so he improvised with a piece of plywood he found in the barn. He was lucky he only broke his collarbone."

She smiled, though she really didn't want to talk

about Seth Dalton. She couldn't seem to shake the memory of that moment she'd awakened and found him examining her.

In her dazed, half-conscious state, she had come dangerously close to wrapping her arms around him and holding on tight. A million sensations had poured through her as his hand touched her ribs, hungers she barely remembered from the early days of her marriage.

She sighed and Jake Dalton gave her a curious look and pressed harder on her shoulder. "Is that a touchy spot?"

"No. Sorry."

"Well, I can't find anything broken. You've got a nasty goose egg where you fell and I suspect a concussion but I'd like to keep a closer eye on that headache for the next hour or so. I'd like you to rest here for a while so I can monitor your head, okay?"

"I've been such a bother."

"You haven't, I promise. I don't want you driving today so your dad is going to take Morgan and Cole home. I'll come check on you in an hour. If you're feeling better at that point, Seth can drive you home."

"I'm fine now."

"I'm sure you are. But you'll have to humor me, okay? It's a doctor thing." He winked at her. "I wouldn't want you to go home too early and drag me out of my warm, cozy bed in the middle of the night if you have any complications. Just rest, okay?"

Her head threatened to throb right off her shoulders and she was exhausted suddenly. She nodded. Closing her eyes gave some relief from the pain anyway.

She awoke some time later to find the room dark except for the flickering fire and next to it a pool of light from a floor lamp of entwined elk antlers. That glow illuminated an entirely too attractive man sitting in an armchair near the fire, a magazine open across his lap and a puppy stretched out at his feet like a pair of fuzzy slippers.

He looked up suddenly as if sensing her gaze. When he saw her eyes open, he gave a slow, painfully sweet smile, and her heart seemed to skip a beat.

"How's the head?" he asked, his voice a low, seductive whisper in the dimly lit room.

As if she could concentrate on anything but him! She closed her eyes for a moment to gauge her pain level then opened to meet his gaze. "Better, I think. Still a bit sore but I'm sure I'll survive. I can tell you with a fairly high degree of certainty that I won't be in a big hurry to go sledding again anytime soon."

He smiled and she felt that same exhilarating, pulse-pounding, toe-curling sensation she'd experienced on the mountain just before she hit that boulder and ruined the ride.

She pulled herself to a sitting position, ignoring the dozens of little elves hammering wildly in her brain. "Has your brother been back?"

"No. He said he'd be here about six and it's only quarter to. You were only asleep for forty-five minutes or so."

"I really think I'm fine to leave now. I just want to go home. I'm sure my father and children are worried about me and I've imposed enough on you and your family."

He closed his magazine and set it on the table beside him, giving her a stern look as he did. "You have any older brothers?"

"No. I'm an only child."

"Ah. Then you have no idea the emotional and psychological torment I would endure if I dared ignore my brother's strict instructions and took you home before he had the chance to take a look at your head again. I'm on strict orders here."

"Do you always do what your older brothers tell you?" she asked.

He gave a snort of laughter. "Hardly ever. Just ask them."

His levity vanished as abruptly as it appeared. "But in this case, I'm not going to take any chances. If Jake thinks you should rest until he checks you out again, that's exactly what you're going to do."

"All this fuss for nothing."

"Nothing? You have no idea how awful it was watching you tumble through the air and hit the ground so hard. I've been having flashbacks about it all evening."

She winced. "It was probably quite a sight, wasn't it?"

"I'd give you an eight for form and a ten for creativity. I'm afraid your bumpy landing knocked down your overall score."

She smiled at his teasing. "I suppose I shouldn't be surprised this happened to me. I faced the painful truth a long time ago. I'm hopelessly uncoordinated. I would have been valedictorian of my class except I never learned to serve a lousy volleyball and couldn't manage to bring my sophomore P.E. grade up past a B."

His laughter rang through the room.

"I'm serious. It's not funny. You have no idea how traumatic it can be for a fourteen-year-old girl who can't shoot a basketball or catch a baseball to save her life."

"I understand. Believe me. You're talking to the kid who was always chosen last for dodgeball teams—and always the first one out."

She studied his athletic build, his broad shoulders and muscled chest and pure masculinity. "Okay, now you're out-and-out lying."

"Ask my brothers! I was small for my age and had asthma. Nobody wanted a shrimp who couldn't breathe on their team."

"You're not a shrimp."

He shrugged. "I hit a growth spurt when I was about Cole's age. Before then I was scrawny."

"Let me guess," she said, with a considering look. "You also started lifting weights around that same time."

"I didn't need to. When you work on a cattle ranch, every day is a workout. Once my asthma was mostly under control, I could do more around the ranch. It's amazing how much a kid can bulk up hauling hay and herding cattle."

She tried to picture him a scrawny, sickly boy suddenly getting taller and bulkier. With those chiseled features and those intense blue eyes that seemed to see right into a woman's deepest desires, he had no doubt always been gorgeous. She imagined when he started to putting on muscle and height, every girl in the county probably sat up and took notice of the youngest Dalton brother.

And they'd been noticing him ever since.

She tilted her head to study him, wondering how much of that late development—coupled with his health issues as a child—had affected his psyche.

"Why are you looking at me like that?" he asked.

She would have liked to be the kind of woman who could instantly sling back some sort of witty repartee. She wanted to be quick and funny and self-assured.

With him gazing at her out of those impossibly blue eyes, with a smile hovering around that sinful mouth, with the lingering scent of leather and pine clinging to him, she couldn't seem to think of anything to say but the truth.

"I was just wondering if that was around the time you discovered you were irresistible to women."

As soon as the words escaped her mouth, she wanted to call them back—or at least pound her head against the coffee table three or four times at her own stupidity.

"Irresistible?" He gave a disbelieving laugh. "Not even close. You, for one, seem to be doing an excellent job of resisting me."

"Am I?"

An arrested look flickered across his features and the room suddenly thickened with tension. Her pulse seemed abnormally loud in her ear and every sense seemed exaggerated. As he continued to gaze at her, she became aware of a hundred different sensations she'd barely noticed before—the slick, cool leather of the couch, the nubby blanket he'd thrown over her, the shadows dancing on the wall from the fire's glow.

She was especially aware of Seth, of his hands strong and square-tipped and masculine, of the slight evening shadow along the curve of his jaw, of the sudden intense light in his eyes.

He seemed big and dangerous and ferociously attractive to her and she wanted to tell him she wasn't anywhere *close* to resisting him.

She couldn't say the words but he seemed to sense them anyway. "This is a mistake," he murmured.

"What is?" she asked, wondering why her lungs couldn't seem to hold a breath.

Before the two words were even out, he gave a low kind of groan that sounded as if he'd lost some kind of internal struggle, then he leaned forward and kissed her.

Oh, he was good at this, she thought as his warm mouth slid gently over hers. Any attempt at overt seduction, an intense or passionate embrace, probably would have sent her spiraling into panic and she would have pulled away.

But his kiss was slow, soft as the purest of silk and incredibly erotic. He touched her with nothing but his mouth, but she still felt surrounded by him, consumed by him.

She should stop this, she thought, for her sanity's sake, if nothing else. But his mouth was so warm and tasted of cinnamon and apples and she felt as if she'd been standing out in the cold forever.

How could he think for an instant she had the capacity to resist him? she wondered. With a sigh of surrender that somehow didn't seem at all like defeat, she returned the kiss, splaying one hand across the soft material of his shirt and winding the other around his neck to tangle her fingers in his thick hair.

He was right about this being a bad idea. She knew it, had done nothing but warn herself of the dangers since the day she met him, but she resolved to worry about that later.

She suddenly thought of her assistant Marcy's theory she'd shared with Ashley that day in the office—The Seth Dalton School of Broncbusting. *Just climb on and hold on tight. It probably won't last too long, but it will be a hell of a ride.*

For now, she would just savor the wild punch of adrenaline, she decided, and enjoy the moment.

Calling this a mistake was a bit like calling the Tetons outside his window a couple of pleasant little hills.

Seth tried to catch his breath, wondering how the hell a simple kiss had so quickly twisted out of his control. He'd only meant to steal one small taste of her, just enough so he wouldn't have to wonder anymore. But the moment his mouth met hers, he felt as if he was the one tumbling head over heels down the mountain out there, as if no matter how he tried he couldn't manage to find his footing in the slippery snow.

He supposed in the back of his mind, he'd thought perhaps they could just share a quick kiss and that would be the end of it. One kiss probably wouldn't have sated his curiosity, but at least it might have been temporarily appeased.

But she had been so soft, so warm and welcoming, and she had given just the tiniest of sighs when he kissed her, and shivered against his mouth.

How could a man resist that?

When she returned his kiss and pulled him closer, he had to use every ounce of strength to keep from pressing her back against the sofa cushions and devouring her. The only way he held himself back was remembering she'd just suffered a head injury and was in no condition for anything more strenuous than a kiss.

When he felt his control fray, he forced himself to pull away, feeling as breathless and lightheaded as he had when he climbed the Grand out there.

In the fire's flickering glow, she looked soft and lovely, like something in one of those watercolors hanging in the Jackson art galleries.

"Have dinner with me tomorrow," he said on impulse. "I know this great place in Idaho Falls."

She gazed at him for several seconds, then she seemed to close up like his mom's flowers at the end of day. She shuttered away all the soft sweetness of her kiss as if it had never been.

"No."

He raised an eyebrow. "Just like that?"

"What else do you need? I know it's probably not a word you're well acquainted with, but I won't have dinner with you. Thank you for asking, though."

He shouldn't have been surprised by the rejection, but after her response to his kiss, he had hoped perhaps she might have changed her mind about him. Obviously, one kiss was not enough to do the trick.

Perhaps he also should have expected the bitter disappointment, but all this seemed uncomfortably foreign.

The silence stretched between them, awkward and uneasy, until finally he spoke, doing his best to keep his voice cool and unaffected.

"Is that a no because you genuinely don't want to, or a no for some other reason?"

She pulled the blanket around her more tightly. "Does it matter?"

"Yeah." More than it should, he admitted to himself. "Humor me. I'd like to know."

She let out a breath. "All right. I'm attracted to you, Seth. I would be lying if I said otherwise."

He frowned. "And yet you say that like it's a bad thing."

"It *is* a bad thing, at least from my perspective. Or if not a bad thing, precisely, at least an impossibility."

"Why?"

She seemed suddenly fascinated by the flickering of the flames. "I'm in a precarious position here. Surely you can see that."

He tried to make sense of what she was talking about but came up empty. "I guess I'm just a big, stupid cowboy," he said. "Why don't you explain it to me?"

"Pine Gulch is a small town. If we—if *I*—gave in to that attraction, people would know. They would talk."

"You're exaggerating a little, don't you think? Who would know or care what you might do in your personal life?"

She shook her head. "You're either incredibly naive—which I find rather hard to believe—or you're being disingenuous. Of course people will care! I'm in a position of trust and responsibility, charged with educating their children! And you are…"

Her voice trailed off but not before he felt his defensive hackles rise. Suddenly he felt ten years old again, on the receiving end of one of Hank's more vicious diatribes. "I'm what?"

She shifted on the couch and refused to meet his gaze. "A favorite topic of conversation around here, for one thing."

"I can't help what people say about me."

"Can't you?"

"What's that supposed to mean?"

She closed her eyes for a moment but when she opened them, they seemed more determined than ever to push him away. "You're a player. You never date a woman more than a few times and you've left a trail of broken hearts strewn across the county. By all accounts, your conquests are the stuff of legend and frankly, I'm not interested in becoming one of them."

She was even better than Jake and Wade at twisting the knife. He wondered if his guts were spilling all over the carpet from that particular jab because it sure as hell felt like it.

"I suppose that's clear enough," he said quietly.

Her eyes darkened and he thought he saw regret there, but he couldn't swear to anything. "I can't afford a complication like this, Seth. Not now. It would be career suicide."

He forced a laugh he was far from feeling. "A little dramatic, don't you think? I only invited you to dinner, not to have wild monkey sex on the front lawn of the school during recess."

She flushed but held her ground. "I can't afford it,"

she repeated. "Surely you can see that. I am perfectly aware that when the school board hired me, some people protested hiring an outsider—and a divorced woman at that. I haven't had time to prove myself yet. If I were to jump into something with you, it will forever define me in the eyes of my faculty and the parents at my school. Those voices who spoke out against hiring me will become a cacophony of protest. I'm trying to build a new life here for me and for my children. I can't risk anything that might threaten that."

He wanted to argue, to find some way around her refusal, but before he could form the torrent of words in his head into anything coherent, the doorbell rang and an instant later, Jake walked into the room without waiting for him to answer it.

Lucy woke up with a start and yipped a welcome.

"Sorry I took a little longer than I'd planned," Jake said, shrugging out of his coat and picking up the puppy. He seemed oblivious to the thick tension in the room, a fact that Seth could only view with gratitude. He was *not* in the mood for another lecture.

On the other hand, he wouldn't mind pounding on something right about now and Jake seemed a convenient target. The only downside to that he could see would be facing the wrath of Magdalena Cruz Dalton, who scared him a whole lot more than her husband.

"Caroline decided she couldn't wait to put her tree up so we were all helping her decorate it and I lost track of time," Jake went on.

"You didn't need to return at all," Jenny said briskly in that prim schoolmarm voice Seth was finding increasingly adorable. "I'm perfectly fine, I promise, and more than ready to go home."

Jake studied her carefully and something in her tone

or her features had him shifting his gaze back to Seth, his eyes suddenly hard. Seth stared back, hating that his brother could make him feel as though he was sixteen years old again.

"She slept most of the time and has only been awake for the past fifteen minutes or so." He hadn't meant to sound defensive but he was very afraid that was how his words came out.

Jake met his gaze for a long moment then turned back to Jenny. "Good. Rest is just what I would prescribe for you. I'm going to recommend taking it easy for the next few days. You're going to feel like you've been hit by a bus at first, but that should only last a day or two."

"All right. Something to look forward to, then," she said, making Jake smile.

"Maggie and I will give you a ride home. We're ready to go back into town and can drop you off with no problem."

Seth started to protest that he wanted to stick to the original plan and be the one to take her home. He would sound ridiculous if he did, he realized, so he opted to keep his mouth shut.

"Thank you," she said without looking at Seth. She managed to avoid his gaze the entire time Jake helped her into her parka and led her toward the door.

He thought she might leave without a word but just before she left, she turned around, her eyes shuttered. "Thank you for inviting us today. My children had a wonderful time."

Her children. Not her.

"I'm sorry it had to end on a sour note," he said.

"So am I," she said, her voice low, and they both knew they weren't talking about her tumble down the mountain. "Goodbye."

He stood on the porch, the icy air cutting through his clothes, as Jake led her down the steps to his waiting Durango. For a long time after their taillights disappeared down the hill, he stood in the cold, watching after them and wondering why *he* was the one who felt as though he'd been hit by a bus.

Chapter Nine

He hadn't missed her. Not a bit.

That was what he tried to tell himself, anyway.

For two weeks, he and Jenny Boyer had successfully managed to avoid each other. Not exactly an easy task in a community as small as Pine Gulch, Idaho.

Now, as Seth drove Cole home after a Saturday spent in the garage working on the GTO, he wondered if this would be the one time he might catch a glimpse of her—or if she would remain frustratingly elusive.

He might not have physically seen her since the day they went hunting Christmas trees on the Cold Creek, but she had never been far from his thoughts.

It was just because she had rejected him, he told himself. She represented the unattainable, the impossible. So naturally, he couldn't focus on anything but her.

For all that he hadn't been able to stop thinking about her, he wasn't completely sure he was all that eager to see her again, not when he was still nursing his wounds from their last encounter. He tended to veer between anger and hurt at the brutal way she had shoved him away after a kiss that to him had been sweetly magical.

She was definitely avoiding him—that much was obvious. The handful of times Cole had come out to the Cold Creek to work on the car or the horses, he had taken the school bus out and his grandfather had picked him up.

She couldn't run from him forever—and she didn't need to. Her message came through loud and clear. He certainly understood rejection when it reached out and slapped him across the face, though that didn't make it any easier to accept.

Cole wound down his monologue about the work they had done on the GTO when they reached the outskirts of town. "Thanks again for giving me a ride," he said.

"No problem. I needed to pick up some things at the store in town anyway."

The only thing in his house was a bottle of Caroline's strawberry jam and a solitary egg and he was out of laundry soap. But he supposed it was safe to admit deep in the recesses of his heart that he'd offered Cole a ride half hoping he might see the boy's mother.

He was pathetic, he thought. What *was* this obsession with her?

This was a pretty miserable way to spend a Saturday night, listening to a teenage boy talk about cars and thinking about his grocery list—and a woman he couldn't have.

So much for her theory that he was some kind of wild-ass cowboy with nothing on his mind but whiskey and women.

Maybe he ought to drop by the Bandito to shake

things up a little before he went grocery shopping. He tried to summon up a little enthusiasm for the idea but the prospect was about as appealing as walking through the grocery store wearing only his Tony Lamas.

Something was seriously wrong with him.

He hadn't avoided the place in the past two weeks, he reminded himself. He had stopped at least two or three times to shoot a little pool, have a couple beers, flirt a little with some pretty girls. But he hadn't enjoyed it much.

Maybe if he tried to enjoy it a little more, expended a little energy and took one of those nice ladies up on their subtle offers, he might not be so edgy and restless, he thought as he drove through the thickening snow. Even as he thought it, he knew he wouldn't.

None of them had soft hair of a hundred different shades and a lush mouth that kept a man up at night.

None of them was Jenny Boyer.

"How much longer before the custom touch-up paint you ordered comes in?" the boy asked.

Seth dragged his mind away from his current dry spell in the romance department and turned his attention to the kid. "They said a week or two. Then all we have to do is give her a couple of coats and we'll be done. Maybe during Christmas break we can take her for a ride, if the weather's not too snowy."

"Yeah. Okay." For all his enthusiasm about working on the GTO, Cole didn't look too thrilled by the idea.

"You've worked hard to pay your debt. I figured when we're done with the touch-up paint, we'll be square. You'll be glad to lift your last shovelfull of horse manure, I'm sure."

"I guess." Cole slumped in the seat and gazed out at the wintry landscape.

He frowned at the almost sullen note of dejection in the boy's voice. Was Cole upset not to be working on the Cold Creek anymore?

He would be sorry to see the last of him. Tinkering with cars had always been a solitary escape for him, but he'd enjoyed having company the last month and Cole had been a different kid when he was working on the GTO, curious and talkative and enthusiastic.

He studied him across the dimly lit truck. "Of course, I wouldn't turn away a hard worker if he wanted to earn a little extra money working with the horses and helping out with the occasional mechanical repair," he said on impulse. "The pay's not the greatest, but you could ride the horses all you want. And in the summer after school gets out, I could probably give you all the hours you wanted to work, provided you would be willing to drive a tractor."

Cole straightened, his features suddenly animated, though he was obviously trying not to show too much excitement. The kid reminded him so much of himself sometimes, watching him was almost painful.

"We'll have to talk to your mom about it," Seth cautioned as he pulled up in front of Jason Chambers's house. "She might prefer you to find an after-school job closer to home."

Cole's enthusiasm wavered a bit but not completely. "We could talk to her now," he suggested. "If you wanted, anyway. I know she must be home since my grandpa went to Jackson Hole yesterday and won't be back until Monday."

Oh, Jenny would love having him show up on her doorstep with an offer like this out of the blue, he thought. But Cole was so eager, he didn't have the heart to refuse.

"Okay," he agreed, anticipation churning through him at knowing he would see her in just a few moments.

He parked his truck in front of the house, noting as
he did that the sidewalk and driveway needed shoveling. Three or four inches had fallen since noon and
several more were forecast before morning.

"I'll talk to your mother with you, on the condition
you help me shovel this snow after we're done."

Cole made a face. "What's the good of shoveling
while it's still snowing? Seems a whole lot smarter to
wait until it stops and then you only have to do it once."

"Here's a little life lesson for you, kid. I know this is
probably your first big storm so you might not have
learned this yet. Most jobs are easier to swallow if you
take them in small bites. Shoveling four inches of snow
three separate times in one storm might seem like a
pain in the neck. But trust me on this, it's a whole lot
easier than waiting until it's all over and having to work
a shovel through two-foot deep drifts."

"Or we could all move somewhere warm so we
wouldn't have to worry about shoveling snow."

"What? And miss all this?" Seth opened the door and
snow swirled inside, icy and cold. The kid rolled his
eyes but climbed out of the passenger side.

Their boots left prints in the snow as they trudged up
the sidewalk through the dark night. He could see the
dark shape of the Christmas tree they'd cut in the
window but the lights hadn't been turned on and neither
were the porch lights.

Odd, he thought.

Cole pushed open the front door. "Mom, I'm home,"
he called. He hit a switch and instantly the tree lit up
with hundreds of colorful lights. It was beautiful, dec-
orated with a hodgepodge of ornaments, most of which
looked homemade. His favorite kind of tree, Seth
thought with satisfaction.

"Mom?" Cole called again.

An instant later, Jenny burst into the room wearing a half-buttoned coat and one glove and holding her car keys in the other hand. She looked frazzled and close to tears.

Her gaze locked on Seth. "Oh, thank heavens! I can't tell you how glad I am to see you."

Seth raised an eyebrow. It wasn't quite the reception he'd expected. He might have made some crack about absence making the heart grow fonder, if she hadn't looked out of her head with worry.

"What's going on?"

"Morgan. She's having a bad flare-up. It's been going on for nearly half an hour and nothing we've tried is helping. I called your brother and he's meeting us at the clinic but I can't get my car started."

"I'll drive you," he said instantly, already moving. "Of course I'll take you! Where is she?"

"In the kitchen."

She led the way and his heart broke when he found Morgan looking terrified and breathing into a nebulizer.

For a moment as he took in her pale features and labored respirations, he was ten years old again, frightened and unable to breathe. He pushed away the ghosts of the past.

"Okay, sweetheart. Asthma-slayers to the rescue here. We're going to get you to Dr. Jake and he'll make everything okay."

He was completely humbled by the absolute and unequivocal trust in her eyes as she nodded.

He scooped her up, blanket and all, and headed back through the house toward the front door and his waiting truck.

After he set Morgan on the seat and fastened her belt, he helped Jenny in after her.

"I've only got three seat belts in my pickup, and I don't dare drive without everyone belted in these road conditions," he said to Cole. "Do you mind staying here?"

"No," he said, looking worried. For all his attitude sometimes, he was just a kid, Seth reminded himself. A boy worried for his sister.

"Don't worry," he said as he went around the truck. "She's tough. Jake will take care of her and she'll be just fine. Meanwhile, your mother and sister would probably appreciate it if they didn't have to trudge through snow to get into the door when we get back."

Cole nodded with a man-to-man kind of look and Seth was pleased to see him already reaching for the snow shovel on the porch.

"I'm very sorry about this," Jenny said as he drove toward the clinic. "I was just about ready to call the ambulance."

"Forget it. We can get her there faster this way, rather than wait for the volunteer paramedics to try to come in to the fire station through the snow."

He had to concentrate on driving for the next few moments as the storm's intensity seemed to increase by the minute. With each passing second, he was aware of Morgan's wheezy struggle to breathe and the huge weight of responsibility pressing down his shoulders.

It gave him some tiny inkling of what parents must go through, this fragile terror at knowing they can sometimes literally hold a child's life in their hands.

When he finally pulled up in front of the clinic, he was sweating through the heavy layers of his coat. He gave a silent prayer of gratitude when he saw Jake's Durango already in the parking lot and all the lights blazing inside.

He scooped Morgan into his arms and headed for the

door, shielding her from the snow with his body. His sister-in-law Maggie was the first one to greet them inside, ready with oxygen and a wheelchair. Jake was right behind her, bustling with the calm competence that made everybody in town trust him with their health.

They both looked surprised to see him there but he didn't waste time in explanations as he set Morgan into the wheelchair then stepped back to let them do their thing.

There was no one on earth he'd rather entrust this sweet little girl to than Jake and Maggie, he thought as he watched them work.

An hour later, Jenny sat beside her daughter's bed in one of the small treatment rooms of the clinic holding Morgan's hand and reading to her from an *American Girl* magazine Seth had found for them in the waiting room while Jake Dalton checked her vitals.

"We seem to be through the worst of it," Jake said now, pulling his stethoscope away from his ears.

"So you think it was her cold that triggered it?" she asked.

"There's a trace of bronchitis there and I'm sure that didn't help anything. My gut tells me it's viral but I'm going to give you some antibiotics anyway, just in case I'm wrong."

"Okay."

"And we'll need to continue the steroid nebulizer treatments every four hours."

"Check."

Jake leaned back against the sink. "Now we have a decision to make and I'm going to leave it up to you. I can ship you to the hospital in Idaho Falls if you would feel better spending the night there."

"Or?"

"I can send you home with a monitor and you can keep on eye on her oxygen levels throughout the night and run the nebulizer treatments on your own. Either way you're probably not going to get any sleep but she might do better in her own bed. If you have problems, I can be at your house in five minutes."

Oh, Jenny absolutely *hated* having to make these decisions on her own. These were the moments she missed having a partner she could count on, someone to lean on during hard times and to help her with these terribly tough calls.

"Are you sure that's wise?" Seth said from the corner. She'd thought he would retreat to the waiting room, but he had stuck around for the whole proceedings, teasing Morgan and asking questions of Maggie and Jake and offering quiet support to Jenny.

She wasn't sure what she would have done without him.

Jake didn't seem upset at the question. "I wouldn't have suggested it as an option if I didn't think she would be fine at home. Since the flare-up is under control, it's probably safer having her in her own bed than trying to transport her through the storm just for observation."

"I want to go home," Morgan said, her voice frail and small. Jenny squeezed her hand, knowing how much her daughter hated hospitals.

"I guess we'll take door number two," she finally said. "I have to think the worst of it has passed."

"I agree. But the only way I'm going to let you take her home is if you promise to call if you have any concerns at all in the night."

Jenny nodded and gave him and Maggie a tired but grateful smile. "Thank you both for meeting us here. I have to confess, one of my biggest worries of moving to a small town so far from a major medical center was finding good care for Morgan's asthma. I never expected to find such wonderful providers in tiny Pine Gulch. I can't tell you what a comfort it is to have you close by."

"You won't find better medical care anywhere," Seth spoke up, his voice gruff. "Pine Gulch is just lucky Jake decided to come home instead of taking one of the big-city offers that came down the pike when he finished medical school. Having an experienced nurse-practitioner like Mag is icing."

His brother looked surprised and touched at the praise, though she thought Seth seemed a little embarrassed after he spoke.

"Well, I'm sorry I had to drag you both out on a night like this."

"It's all part of the job description," Maggie assured her. "Don't give it a thought."

After Jake rounded up an oxygen-saturation monitor, Maggie brought a wheelchair for them to use to transport Morgan out to the truck, but Seth shook his head.

"I've got it," he said, wrapping the little girl in a blanket and lifting her into his arms again.

He had pulled his truck right up to the door so only had to take a few steps through the blowing snow to set her inside carefully.

Jenny's heart seemed to shift and settle as she watched this big, overwhelmingly masculine man take such gentle care with her child. Morgan gave him a sleepy smile as he fastened her seat belt and Jenny had to swallow her sigh.

Her daughter was already crazy about Seth. This little episode wasn't going to do anything to diminish her hero worship. She desperately hoped her daughter wouldn't have her heart broken by another male in her life.

Exhausted by her ordeal, Morgan fell asleep before they even made it out of the parking lot.

Seth drove with native confidence through the miserable conditions. At least a foot had fallen since the storm had started earlier in the evening and most of it was still on the roads, but he hardly seemed to notice it.

At her father's house, she was surprised to see all but a skiff of snow had been cleared from the driveway. She frowned. Who could have done it? She could only hope Jason hadn't driven home in these conditions from Jackson Hole.

Maybe a neighbor, she thought as she followed Seth and Morgan inside. She was discovering people in Pine Gulch took care of each other. It was another reason she desperately wanted to make things work out for them here. She loved being part of a community, a small part of the greater whole.

"Where am I heading?" Seth whispered inside the welcome warmth of the house. Morgan was still sleeping, she saw.

"Her room," she whispered back. "I'll show you."

She led the way to Morgan's room, across the hall from her own and he set her carefully down on the bed.

"Thank you," she murmured, aware of him watching her intently as she hooked up the monitor then drew the quilt up over Morgan's sleeping form.

In the living room, they found Cole waiting for them, trying hard not to look worried.

"How is she?" he asked.

"Better. Good enough that Dr. Dalton seemed to think she'd be all right at home tonight," Jenny said.

She was suddenly exhausted after the last two hours of stress and she could feel an adrenaline crash coming on.

"Good job clearing the walks and the driveway," Seth said.

She stared at her son. "You did that?"

He stuck out his jaw. "Yeah. So?"

She sighed, wondering how she always seemed to say exactly the wrong thing to him. She decided to use actions instead of words and pulled him into a hug. "Thank you."

In a rare and precious gift, he let her hug him for a long moment before he stepped away.

"You're supposed to call Grandpa. He said he can come home if you need him."

"I don't want him driving in this mess. But I also don't want to be stuck here without transportation if Morgan has a relapse."

"You won't be without transportation," Seth put in. "You'll have my truck."

She frowned. "If you leave your truck, what will you use to get back to the Cold Creek?"

"Nothing. Not tonight, anyway. I'm bunking on your couch."

Chapter Ten

As he might have expected, Jenny was less than enthusiastic about his declaration.

Sparks seemed to shoot out of her suddenly narrowed eyes and the look she gave him plainly did not bode well for him. She opened her mouth—to flay him alive, no doubt—then cast a look at Cole and closed it again. He had never been so grateful for her son's presence.

"I appreciate the offer," she said tightly, "but that's really not necessary. I'm sure you have plenty of other places you would rather be on a stormy night like tonight."

"Nope," he said, and was astonished to realize it was true.

Something was definitely wrong with him. This was usually his favorite kind of night, stormy and cold, the kind of night designed for cuddling up under a warm quilt with a sweet young thing, putting his mind to work coming up with imaginative ways to keep warm.

Why did that seem so totally unappealing to him right now? He would far rather be here in Jason Chambers's house with a woman who wanted nothing to do with him, sleeping alone on a cold couch.

"Jenny, there's no way under the sun I'm going to leave you alone here tonight and that's the end of it. I would never sleep worrying about Morgan and about you stuck here without wheels in this weather. I don't mind the couch."

The phone rang suddenly in the kitchen and though he looked loath to leave this interesting battlefield, Cole went to answer it.

Jenny cast a quick look through the doorway to make sure her son couldn't overhear, then she spoke in a low voice. "You can't stay here. It's impossible. What would people think if your truck were parked out front all night?"

For one near-disastrous second, he almost laughed, but she seemed so serious, so genuinely distressed, the impulse died, leaving a hollow feeling in his gut.

She wasn't joking. She was so concerned about her reputation, she thought just the sight of his truck parked out front of her house all night would destroy it.

He had no idea what it was like to be a pillar of society—and he wasn't sure he wanted to know, especially if it meant worrying about something that seemed so inconsequential to him.

Did she really think anybody would believe the elementary school principal would invite the town's bad boy over for a night of wild sex while her children were in the house?

He had to admit, the thought of that soft body of hers all warm and cuddly was far too appealing under the circumstances, but he managed to rein in his overactive imagination.

"Nobody's going to be out in this weather to be snooping on the neighbors," he assured her. "All the town busybodies are tucked up in their beds dreaming of catching the mayor's wife shoplifting or something. And if anybody's rude enough to ask, we can just tell them the truth. Or if you don't think that's good enough, we can always tell them I loaned my truck to you when your car broke down."

She didn't look convinced. "It's the ones who *won't* say anything who worry me most. Those are the kinds of whispers that can destroy a reputation in an instant."

He couldn't have said why it bothered him so much that she was so concerned about her precious reputation—or that she seemed so convinced he held the power to completely destroy it.

"You really care about the opinions of some old biddies with nothing better to do than bad-mouth a woman whose only crime is worrying about her sick child?"

"It's not that simple."

"What's your alternative? Dragging your father home from Jackson Hole in this weather? I know you don't want to do that."

"No. There must be some other solution."

"Not that I can see. I'm staying, Jen. You don't know stubborn until you've taken on a Dalton."

She opened her mouth to answer but Cole appeared in the doorway, looking from one of them to the other out of curious eyes. He held out a black cordless phone. "Grandpa's on the phone again, Mom."

She took it from him and Cole disappeared. A moment later, Seth heard his tread on the stairs and assumed the boy had retreated to his room.

While Jenny was on the phone, Seth took off his coat and hung it on a hall tree in the entryway, then returned to the living room. Jenny'd had the same idea—she'd taken off her hat and scarf and her coat and tossed them over a chair.

"No, Dad. I don't want you to come home," she said, unbuttoning her cardigan to reveal a formfitting forest green turtleneck underneath. She slipped out of the sweater, and Seth slid onto the couch and stretched his legs out in front of him, enjoying himself immensely.

She narrowed her eyes at his comfortable pose. "There's nothing you can do. Nothing *anyone* can do," she added with a pointed look at Seth.

He smiled benignly, wondering how much more she might be planning to take off.

"All right. I'll call you if there's any change, I promise. Yes. Okay. Stay safe. Have fun with your friends and don't lose too much money. I know. You always win. That's why you go. All right. I love you, too, Dad."

She hung up from her father, set the phone on the coffee table and stood gazing at her bright Christmas tree, looking so dejected Seth almost offered to go find a nice, respectable widow with her own snowplow if it would make Jenny feel better about the situation.

After a moment, she straightened her shoulders and faced him. He suddenly wanted more than anything to take that grim look out of her eyes, to make everything okay.

"Your dad is obviously a cardsharp, but how are *you* at poker?" he asked.

She blinked, looking a little disoriented. "Sorry?"

"We're going to be up all night worrying about Morgan and giving her treatments every four hours, but we don't have to be bored. Let's call Cole up to play some cards. What do you say? We can play for pennies or toothpicks or matchsticks or whatever you've got. Unless you think we'd be corrupting the morals of a minor."

Her laugh was abrupt, but he took comfort that it was still a laugh. "Are you kidding? My dad taught him to play blackjack the minute he was old enough to count. He'll wipe the floor with both of us."

"Speak for yourself, ma'am. You've never played cards with me. I don't like to lose."

She sniffed. "I believe I've figured that out by now."

He laughed, glad that he'd been able to distract her, if only for a moment.

Where was her child?

Jenny raced through the halls of an unfamiliar hospital, her way strewn with gurneys and hospital equipment and hallways that led nowhere.

She opened every door but couldn't find Morgan anywhere. Somewhere in this labyrinthian hell was her child, ill and wheezy, but Jenny had no idea where to look. Her baby needed her and she wasn't there for her.

She begged everyone she passed to please help her, but no one answered. No one at all. Finally, when she was nearly wailing with defeat, she headed down one last, crowded hallway, devoid of doors except for one at the very end, lit by a strange orange glow from within.

Her child had to be there, she thought, trying to shove her way past uncaring people who blocked her at every turn. She felt so alone, so utterly forsaken. She was so tired of fighting this battle by herself. All she wanted was to curl up and weep out all her pain and frustration, but she had to find her child.

Suddenly—like a miracle, like the parting of the Red Sea—a path opened up for her through the crowd of people. Someone stood in front of her, someone with shoulders broad enough to carry the weight of all her fears. She couldn't see his face, but her salvation blazed a trail for her and she rushed toward the door. When she reached it, she extended a hand to thank the only person who had helped her.

He turned and gave her a slow, painfully sweet smile and opened the door for her. Somehow she had known it was Seth, she thought, even as she rushed inside to her child, sobbing with relief to find her healthy and whole, her breathing slow and even.

She awoke with a start, disoriented by the strange dream.

She wasn't sure where she was at first, then she realized the orange glow she had dreamed about must have been from the woodstove, where a fire still flickered softly.

She was in her father's den, curled up on the couch. She frowned, trying to remember why she'd fallen asleep there, then the lingering tendrils of her dream wrapped around her again and she drew in a quick breath.

Morgan!

Jenny yanked off the soft knitted afghan she couldn't remember pulling around herself and rose so quickly the room whirled for a moment. She barely waited for the walls to steady before rushing down the hall to her daughter's room, her heart pounding.

All was quiet there. The alarm clock by the bed told Jenny she'd slept longer than she thought—it was nearly quarter after four. How could she have fallen asleep when her daughter needed her?

But no. A quick check told her Morgan was sleeping soundly. The oxygen monitor on her bedside table registered a respectable ninety-four. Not fabulous but not terrible, either.

She let out a low sigh of relief and lifted a trio of

stuffed animals from the glider rocker by Morgan's bed so she could take their place.

Her daughter was due for another nebulizer treatment and though Jenny hated to wake her, she knew it was something neither of them could avoid.

Poor little thing, to have to endure so much, she thought, as she poured the medicine into the nebulizer then shook her awake.

"I'm sorry, sweetheart, but you need a treatment."

Morgan groaned but blinked her eyes open blearily, just long enough for Jenny to fit the mask over her nose and mouth and turn on the machine. Medicated air blew into the mask, forcing its way into her daughter's lungs. Morgan hated that part, she knew.

"Do you want me to hold you?" she asked.

Morgan nodded, so Jenny slid into bed with her, cuddling her tight and singing softly to her until the medicine was finished.

She settled Morgan back into bed and was grateful when she closed her eyes and slipped easily back to sleep.

Perhaps because of the silly dream and the remembered terror of not being able to find her, Jenny stood for a long time by her daughter's bed, thinking how very much she loved her. Despite what she sometimes had to endure, Morgan was warm and good-natured. An uncommonly kind child, she often thought.

She couldn't imagine how cold and lonely her life would have been without either of her children.

Cole might be struggling through his teenage years but she wouldn't trade him for anything. As she finally left Morgan's room, she couldn't help thinking of the evening she, Seth and Cole had spent together and she had to smile.

She didn't know how Seth had done it, but somehow

in the course of the night while they played Five-Card Stud and Acey-Deucy and Texas Hold 'em, he had returned her funny, sweet son to her.

She knew it was probably fleeting, that in the morning Cole would likely revert to his normal sullen, unhappy self. But for a few hours he had laughed and joked and teased with her and—miracle of miracles— had even seemed to enjoy her company.

Around midnight, Cole had been drooping over his cards so Jenny sent him to bed. She had been loath to say good-night to him, both because she had so enjoyed her time with him and because she desperately needed the buffer he provided between her and Seth.

She needn't have worried. While she woke Morgan for her midnight treatment, Seth apparently had thumbed through her father's DVD collection until he found an old Alfred Hitchcock movie, one of her favorites.

"I haven't seen this in years," he exclaimed when she returned to the den after that treatment earlier. "What do you think? Are you up to watching a movie?"

She had agreed and had tried to stay awake, but the long, arduous evening of worry and caregiving took its toll. She didn't think she had made it very far through the movie.

Now the TV was dark and her unwanted houseguest was nowhere in sight. Had he gone home? She hurried to the window but there was his big black pickup truck, looking dark and menacing and incriminating against the snow.

He must have decided to go to bed. It couldn't have been too long before she woke up, as the log in the woodstove still looked fresh and barely burned through.

How long had she been out of it while he sat watching the movie? she wondered. She felt curiously vulnerable knowing she must have slept in front of him. It was a disconcerting thing to realize another person might have watched her sleep—especially when that person was a man she found enormously attractive.

Where was he now? Some hostess she was, whether or not her guest was an invited one. Perhaps he had found an empty bed to stretch out on, either in her room or her father's.

She should at least check to see if he had found somewhere to rest. If her guest was awake, a good hostess should at least ascertain if he needed anything.

Her pulse kicked up as a heated image jumped into her mind of wild kisses and tangled limbs.

No! She only meant a clean towel or a spare toothbrush.

She did her best to push the fiery images away but they haunted her as she paused outside her father's bedroom. No light shone underneath the door but she was still cautious as she pushed it open, only to release a heavy breath when she found an empty bed.

He must have gone to her room, then. Her stomach fluttered as she pictured that long, powerful body stretched out on her bed. Her pillow would smell like him, she thought. Leathery and masculine and delicious.

She stood outside the door, her stomach twisting with nerves. She rolled her eyes at her reaction. This was ridiculous. He was only a man, for heaven's sake. Just a man who was probably snoring up a storm right now.

Still, she felt a little like Pandora lifting the lid of her box as she pushed open her bedroom, then slumped against the door.

He wasn't there, either. Her bed was just as she had left it that morning, the corners neat and the pillow shams aligned.

Completely baffled now, she returned to the kitchen.

He had to be *somewhere* in the house. She was about to check if he had somehow managed to find her father's guest room in the basement when she heard a clatter on the other side of the door leading to the garage, then a muffled curse.

For the first time, she noticed a narrow slice of light under the door. She frowned. The garage? What on earth would Seth be doing in the *garage* at four-thirty in the morning?

Shaking her head in confusion, she pushed open the door and shivered as a blast of cold air slapped at her.

She heard whistling first, some tune she couldn't name but that she suspected was on the bawdy side. She followed the sound and nearly tumbled down the two small steps leading into the garage at what she saw.

The hood of her little SUV was open and Seth was bent over fiddling with something under it.

She couldn't seem to take her eyes off him as she tried to process what he was doing. It was hours before dawn and he was out in below-freezing weather in the middle of a blizzard working on her car.

This was the man she thought was an immature womanizer interested in only one thing, the man she wouldn't go to dinner with for fear someone might see them and her job might be threatened, the man she had rejected a dozen different ways.

Why would he do such a thing?

Something seemed to break loose inside of her, something precious and tender and terrifying, and she pressed a hand to her mouth, shaken to her soul.

She must have made some sound because the whistling broke off in midnote and he peered his head around the side of her hood. When he saw her, he gave her one of those heartbreaking smiles of his.

"Hi!" he said cheerfully.

She couldn't think of anything to say, lost in the tumult of emotions washing through her.

At her continued silence, his smile slipped away. "Is everything okay with Morgan? I checked on her a while ago and everything seemed fine, I swear, or I would have woken you."

She had to force herself to speak, if only to allay his worry. "She is. Her oxygen levels are still within normal range and I just gave her another nebulizer treatment. As soon as she finished the last of it, she went right back to sleep, just like she did at midnight."

She didn't trust herself to say anything more just now, too stunned by his actions.

"That's wonderful," he said fervently.

She walked down the steps until she stood only a few feet away from him. "Seth, what are you doing here?"

He gave a little laugh that seemed to run down her spine like a warm caress. "A little self-evident, don't you think?"

"It's four-thirty in the morning! You should be home in bed, not standing in my ice-cold garage monkeying under my hood."

He raised an eyebrow and by the sudden amusement in his eyes, she realized how her words could be taken as a euphemism.

Why did men have to turn so much having to do with automobiles and their maintenance into sexual double entendres? *Lube her chassis, rotate her tires, give the old engine a tune-up.* And of course, all engines were female, the better for them to work their wiles.

To her relief, Seth didn't make any smart remark, though—he just smiled. "It was no big deal. I just didn't want you being stuck here tomorrow if your father doesn't make it back from Jackson because of the weather. Anyway, I'm just about done. Let's see if my monkeying did the trick."

He slid behind the wheel and turned the key he must have found on her key ring in the kitchen. The engine started up instantly, practically purring in the cold garage.

"Of course," she muttered to herself. Just like everything else female the man touched.

Seth slid out with a satisfied smile. "There you go. She's all ready to rock."

Oh, she was in serious trouble.

"What was my problem?" she managed to ask. *Besides this foolish, foolish heart?*

"Corrosion around the battery cables. I only cleaned her up a little with some baking soda and water. But then I saw by the sticker on your windshield you were past due for an oil change and discovered your dad happened to have five quarts of the right grade oil, so I decided to take care of that, too. No big deal."

"It's a very big deal to me," she murmured. She couldn't remember the last time anyone had performed such a gesture for her. Against her will, she thought of the nightmare she'd had just before she awoke, of feeling helpless and alone and terribly frightened. And then he was there, lending her his strength when she had none of her own left.

"I'm just glad you won't be left without a car now," he said, wiping his hands on one of the rags from a box her father kept in the corner.

She leaned closer. "You've got a smudge on your face."

"Yeah, I always make a mess when I'm working on a car."

He scrubbed it without success. Without thinking, she

took the rag from him and stepped forward, carefully wiping at the small spot of grease just above his jawline.

An instant later, she realized what she was doing and she stopped, mortified. Her gaze slid to his and the sudden heat there seemed to burn through her, setting every nerve ending ablaze.

She swallowed hard and thought she might have whispered his name, but it was lost in the wild firestorm of his kiss.

Chapter Eleven

His arms wrapped around her, tangling her up in a heat and strength that smelled vaguely of motor oil and sexy male.

She clung tightly to his shirt and slid into the wonder of his kiss. He was so good at it, his mouth teasing and tasting until she couldn't seem to grab hold of a single coherent thought.

A corner of her mind protested that she played a risky game. This was crazy, foolish. A smart woman should be running for all she was worth from the heartbreak he would inevitably leave behind, not reaching out to grab it with both hands.

She knew it, but she couldn't let herself think about that now, when his mouth was so warm and exhilarating, with his hard strength beneath her fingertips, with her heart still reeling from the magnitude of what he had just done for her.

The cold and rather drab garage seemed to disappear. Her SUV, her father's power tools, the snow still whirling outside the window. Nothing existed but the two of them, this man who seemed to know her so well, who somehow reached into her deepest dreams and gave her a reality far more magical than anything she could have imagined.

She felt safe in his arms. It was an odd thought—one she didn't quite understand, considering he was the most dangerous man she'd ever met. At least to her emotions.

At this moment, though, as his mouth explored hers and his arms held her tightly, she felt protected from the cold and storms of life, as if he would safeguard her from any threat.

She didn't know how long the kiss lasted. Time seemed to have no meaning, elastic and malleable. Einstein's theory of relativity held new meaning when a woman found herself in Seth Dalton's arms.

When at last she came up for air, they were both breathing hard and she wondered if she looked as dazed as he did.

"Wow," he said, his voice ragged. "That's one hell of a tip just for cleaning off a little battery corrosion."

She flushed and tried to retreat, but he wouldn't let her, pulling her close until she fitted snugly against him. His heat surrounded her, taking away the chill from the cold garage.

"I should *not* have done that," she murmured, though with him so close, crowding out all her good sense, it wasn't easy to hang on to all the reasons why.

"If you're looking for me to agree with you on that particular point, I'm afraid you're going to be doomed to disappointment."

What must he think of her? She had been an idiot

around him, weak and mercurial, since the day they met. Like now, for instance. She knew she shouldn't be so content in the circle of his arms but she couldn't manage the strength to pull away.

"I have no willpower where you're concerned. I'm sorry."

His arms tightened around her. "Sweetheart, you have nothing to apologize about."

She drew in a deep breath and summoned all her strength so she could force herself to step out of that warm haven. "Yes, I do. I've done nothing but give you mixed signals about what I want since that first day you came to the house with Cole. I tell you I'm not interested, then I attack you like some kind of…of sex-starved divorcée."

That masculine dimple appeared briefly. "Are you?"

Yes. *Oh, yes,* at least where this man was concerned. A few weeks ago she would have laughed at the notion that she could be so hungry. She hadn't had a physical relationship since her divorce, hadn't even considered one until Seth—and hadn't noticed the lack of it.

She had devoted all her energy and time to her children and her career. No man had even tempted her until Seth blew into her life with his sexy smile and his broad shoulders and those eyes that seemed to see right into her deepest desires.

Oh, yes. She was starving and he was like a big, gluttonous, delectable feast.

"You're blushing," he observed.

She felt herself flush even hotter and didn't know how to respond to his teasing.

"I'm trying to apologize for the mixed signals. I'm just…I'm not very good at all of this."

"This?"

"We have this…thing between us. I don't know what to do with it. I thought keeping a safe distance was the answer, but that obviously isn't working."

"No?"

"Even though I know perfectly well you're so bad for me, I can't seem to stop thinking about you."

At her words, something hot and intense sparked in his eyes. Perhaps she ought not have mentioned that last part, she thought nervously.

"Why am I so terrible?" he asked. "Because you think the whole town will start a riot if they should find out the elementary school principal might actually want a life?"

A life was one thing. A torrid affair with the town's hottest bachelor was something else entirely.

"You're out of my league, Seth. Way, way out of my league. I'm like the water boy on a Pop Warner football team and you're the starting quarterback in the Superbowl."

"Sorry, but baseball was my game."

"You know what I mean. I don't even know why you're here. You're a…a *player.* You're sexy and exciting and gorgeous. And I'm just a boring, dumpy thirty-six-year-old elementary school principal who has slept with exactly one man in my entire life."

Oh, she shouldn't have said that, either. His gaze sharpened and she could swear he saw right into her soul.

"Really?" he asked in an interested voice.

She flushed. "That's beside the point. What I'm trying to say is I can't figure any of this out. What do you want from me, Seth? I know perfectly well I'm not your usual type. I'm not beautiful or sexy or exciting. I've never been the kind of person who's always the life of the party. I'm just an ordinary woman, someone a man like you shouldn't even look twice at."

He looked astonished at her blunt self-assessment. "How can you say that with a straight face?"

"Because it's true!"

"I don't think you know yourself very well," he murmured. "And I'm certain you don't know me."

She couldn't argue with that. If she knew him, perhaps he wouldn't baffle her so completely.

"You seem to think I'm some rowdy cowboy with nothing on my mind but carving notches on some imaginary bedpost," he went on. "I'll admit, I have a bit of a reputation. Some of it earned, I'm sorry to say, but most of it exaggerated."

He was quiet for a moment, and then he gave her a solemn look, more serious than she'd ever seen from him. "But you know, there's more to me than whatever reputation I might have."

She wrapped her arms around herself, struck by his words. He was right. How unfair had she been to him, to hang everything on some whispered gossip overheard in her office?

He was more than what people said about him. She only had to look at what he had done for her little family in the last month to see the truth of that.

He had been wonderful to Cole, patient and kind and understanding when most other men would have ranted and raved and pressed charges, more concerned about the damages to their prize automobile than about a troubled boy.

And Morgan adored him. He had shown extraordinary gentleness and rare perception to her daughter, and for that she would never be able to thank him enough. If nothing else, he'd shown her daughter it was possible to move past the frustrating limitations of asthma to have a successful, rewarding life as an adult.

She thought of his steady strength during Morgan's flare-up. They had all been so frightened, but Seth hadn't hesitated for an instant, had stepped into the breach and helped them all find their way through it.

If she needed further confirmation there were deeper levels to him than the world might see, she only had to look at his relationship with his family. The Daltons were a close and loving group and he seemed crazy about them all.

He had no problems hugging his mother in public, he plainly adored his niece and nephews, he was passionate about his horses.

And he had been willing to come out to a cold garage in the middle of a stormy winter night to fix her car so she wouldn't be stranded.

She hadn't wanted to see all those good things about him, she realized. It was far easier to use his wild reputation as a shield to keep him away—and to keep her heart safe.

Continuing to focus on that one aspect of him was doing both of them an injustice.

"I know there's more to you," she finally admitted. "Perhaps that's why I can't stop thinking about you."

At her low words, a soft and tender warmth stole through him and he couldn't seem to stop looking at her in the dim light of the garage.

How could she actually say she wasn't beautiful? Just now, with her mouth swollen and her eyes still heavy-lidded from their kiss, he had never seen such a stunning sight. She looked rumpled and warm and he wanted her with a ferocity that astonished him.

For now, he contented himself with simply reaching for her hand. "I don't know if this helps anything," he finally said, "but I can't stop thinking about you, either. This sounds crazy, I know, but somehow I missed you these last few weeks. You told me to back off and I've tried to respect that. But I couldn't get you out of my head."

Her hand trembled in his. "How could you miss me? You don't even know me. Not really."

"I don't know the answer to that, I just know it's true. I'd like to know you, Jenny. Just as I'm more than my wild reputation, you're more than the boring, ordinary educator you see in the mirror. I know you are. You're beautiful and smart and funny."

She looked as if she wanted to protest but he didn't give her the chance. "I think we owe each other the chance to see beyond the surface."

"Seth—"

"Have dinner with me. Just one date. That's all I'm asking," he pressed. "One evening without all this tension and conflict that doesn't have to be there. There's this great restaurant I know in Jackson Hole. Neutral territory. We won't see anybody we know and we can talk and laugh and enjoy each other's company. I'll even promise to keep my hands to myself, if that's what it will take."

It just might be the toughest promise he ever had to keep, he thought, but he could handle it if it offered him the chance to bust through all her roadblocks.

She slipped her hand from his and wrapped her arms around herself. His heart sank and he braced himself for one more rejection from her, knowing somehow this one would hurt worse than all the others combined after that tender kiss they had just shared.

He saw the indecision in her eyes, then her gaze shifted from him to her car for just a moment. He had no idea what she saw there, but when she looked back, he was stunned to see the uncertainty replaced by something soft and warm, something that left him breathless.

"All right. Yes. I'll go to dinner with you."

He wasn't at all prepared for the raw emotion that coursed through him at her words—a tangle of joy and relief and elation. It left him more than a little uneasy, but he resolved not to worry about that now.

How had things come to this?

Ten days later, just a week before Christmas, Jenny pulled out the roast chicken to check it one final time. The skin looked perfect, crisp and golden, and the whole kitchen was redolent with delicious smells—fresh rolls, creamy mashed potatoes and the succulent chicken.

"Does this look right?" Morgan asked from the kitchen island where she was drizzling chocolate syrup across the cheesecake she'd made earlier in the day.

"Delicious," she assured her daughter, who unfortunately had inherited her somewhat less-than-gourmet skills in the kitchen.

"Do you think Seth will like it?"

"Will like what?" the man in question asked from the doorway and her heart gave its customary foolish little leap.

She really needed to have a talk with her father about letting Seth into the house without giving her some kind of warning so she could brace herself for his impact on her.

How was it possible he was more gorgeous every time she saw him? she wondered. Tonight he wore faded jeans, worn boots and a burgundy fisherman's sweater that made her mouth water. Throw in that heartbreaking smile and the sweet little puppy cavorting around his legs and it was no wonder she had no defenses against him.

She cleared her throat. "Hi," she said.

His smile widened and she wondered how he could consume every oxygen particle just by walking into a room.

"Hi." His greeting encompassed both of them, but the light in his eyes was entirely for her, she knew, though she didn't understand it and couldn't quite believe it.

"What will I like?"

"Morgan made you a dessert," Jenny said. "She's a little worried you won't like it."

"You made that?"

He walked closer, bringing with him the clean, masculine scent of his aftershave. He smelled far better than anything she'd fixed for dinner and all she wanted to do was devour him.

She forced herself to take several deep, cleansing breaths to calm down as Morgan nodded with a grimace.

"It's kind of uneven," her daughter admitted. "I was hoping the chocolate syrup would hide it."

"Are you kidding? It looks like something out of a magazine. I hope nobody else is hungry because I just might have to eat that whole thing all by myself."

Morgan giggled, her eyes glowing. Jenny knew she must look the same.

How had things come to this? She had no willpower where the man was concerned.

What had started out as one simple dinner invitation to one of the more exclusive Jackson Hole restaurants had somehow slid into a regular event in the last ten days.

She had seen him nearly every day since the night he'd helped with Morgan's flare-up and fixed her car. They had gone to dinner twice in Jackson Hole, had taken the kids to a movie in Idaho Falls one day, had taken a drive to Mesa Falls to watch the spectacular show of water thrusting through ice.

They'd even gone for a snowy moonlit horseback ride on the ranch—which might have been romantic if they hadn't had both Natalie and Morgan along, chattering all the way.

It was after that horseback ride two nights before when they'd been sipping hot cocoa by his soaring Christmas tree that she'd taken the huge step of asking him to dinner.

She hadn't meant to—had actually been working up to telling him she couldn't see him anymore. But the invitation had slipped from her subconscious to her tongue before she knew it.

She couldn't take it back, especially when he had looked so delighted. It was the first time she had initiated a social encounter between them and she knew he must have realized that fact as well as she did.

As wonderful as she had to admit these ten days had been, she wasn't quite sure where things stood between them. Despite the wild heat of that night in the garage, they hadn't shared anything like that since. He was true to his word, she had discovered. When he said he would keep his hands to himself, he meant exactly that.

Though he was attentive and courteous, any physical contact between them was casual—a hand on her arm to help her over an icy patch, fingers casually laced through hers in a darkened theater as they watched a movie, a barely-there good-night kiss when he dropped her off after dinner.

If he meant to drive her crazy with lust, he was certainly succeeding. She was a quivering mass of hormones when he was around.

They couldn't keep on like this.

The thought crawled through her mind again, stark and depressing. Seeing him was accomplishing nothing except giving her this wild hunger for something she knew she couldn't have.

"Anything I can do?" Seth asked.

She pushed away the thought for now and mustered a smile. "I think we're there, aren't we, Morgan?"

Her daughter nodded.

"We only have to take the food into the dining room."

"I can't even begin to tell you how delicious everything looks," he murmured, and her whole body seemed to shiver and sigh. He was looking at *her* and not the dinner she'd spent so much time preparing.

"Here," she said abruptly, thrusting a dish to him. "You can carry in the bird."

He grinned as if he knew exactly his effect on her, but took the tray from her and headed out of the kitchen.

After he left, Jenny turned to find Morgan watching, a curious light in her eyes. Her daughter waited about ten seconds before she spoke in a voice pitched low. "Are you going to marry Seth?"

The bowl of mashed potatoes slipped from Jenny's suddenly nerveless fingers and she had to scramble to keep them from splattering all over the kitchen floor.

"No! Wherever did you get that idea?"

"You like him though, don't you?"

Heaven spare her from nine-year-old girls who saw entirely too much. "I…yes. Of course I do. But that's a far cry from marrying him, honey. We're only friends."

Morgan digested that, looking a little disappointed. "I just wanted you to know I wouldn't mind. I don't think Cole would, either. He's a lot nicer when Seth is around."

"Okay. Um, good to know." This wasn't a conversation she wanted to have right now, with Seth just on the other side of that wall. She could only pray he didn't come back in.

"Natalie says it's pretty cool having a stepparent. Mrs. Dalton is way nice to her and fixes her hair and everything."

"You already have someone to fix your hair," she pointed out, hoping to distract her. "Me!"

"I know. But I don't have someone to teach me how to ride horses or who knows what I feel like when my asthma flares." Morgan was quiet for a moment. "You laugh a lot more when Seth is here. So if you want to marry him, I wouldn't mind."

Her daughter picked up the cheesecake she put such effort into and carried it out of the kitchen.

When she left, Jenny pressed a hand to her mouth. Oh, she needed to put a stop to this. She should have realized how Morgan would construe the fragile beginnings of whatever this was with Seth. He was the only man she had spent any time with socially since the divorce, so it was logical for Morgan to jump to the wrong conclusion.

Shaking him loose was going to hurt.

The knowledge left a cold knot in her stomach. It would hurt, but not as much as they would all hurt if she let things continue as they were.

He wasn't serious about her. She still didn't know why exactly he seemed to want to spend so much time with her, but she knew he couldn't possibly have anything lasting in mind.

"Are we eating or are we going to sit here looking at all this pretty food all night?" her father called from the dining room.

"I'm coming. Sorry."

She let out a breath, then grabbed the rolls and the

salad. Tonight. She had to find some way to tell him this had to be the end of it.

No matter how much she loved being with him, how the whole world seemed more vivid and wonderful whenever he was near, she had to stop indulging herself before her children opened their hearts and their lives to him any further.

And before she did the same.

Chapter Twelve

Forty-five minutes later, she was no closer to figuring out how she was going to force herself to end something that seemed so perfect—though with each passing moment, she knew she had no choice.

Seth set down his fork with a sigh of satisfaction. "Ladies, that was just about the best dinner I've had in longer than I can remember. Especially the cheesecake."

Morgan beamed, clearly smitten. "It's my mom's recipe. I just followed the directions."

"Even though you had a great recipe to start with, you were the one who did such a good job following it. But kudos to your mom, too."

"I can't really take credit," Jenny protested. "I always just use the recipe that comes on the cream cheese package—nothing very original, I'm afraid."

He laughed. "Enough of this humility! Will somebody please accept the compliment?"

"I will," Cole offered with a grin.

Everyone laughed, since Cole had had absolutely nothing to do with the cheesecake except eating a hefty slice.

As the laughter faded, Jenny looked around the table, a bittersweet pang in her chest. Her children would be hurt when Seth stopped coming around. Would Cole and Morgan understand why she had to send him packing? Or would they blame her for it?

"I need to move after that big meal," Seth said with a smile. "Anybody feel like taking a walk? I figured we could walk the few blocks to downtown and judge for ourselves which house ought to win the town's holiday lighting contest."

"I want to!" Morgan exclaimed.

Cole shrugged but didn't seem opposed to the idea. Or if he was, at least he didn't roll his eyes or say it blew.

"Jen? Jason? What about you two?"

"I have to finish the dishes," Jenny stalled, despising herself for her cowardice.

She had yet to go anywhere in town with Seth where others might see them together.

Though she knew they always stood the chance of running into someone from Pine Gulch in Jackson or Idaho Falls, she'd convinced herself the likelihood of that was slim.

On the other hand, even if someone *did* see them tonight as they walked through town, what would be the harm in enjoying the holiday sights with him accompanied by the rest of her family?

Her father slid his chair back from the table and started to clear away dishes. "You all go have some fun. I'll clean up."

"The kitchen's a disaster," she said. "You know what a mess I make when I cook."

Her dad only smiled. "Well, you *are* the only person I know who can dirty three or four pans just boiling water for pasta. But I think I'm up to the task. Go on."

He used that implacable "don't argue" voice and she sighed. She could have used a little backup, but she didn't think she would find it from her father. At least not in this instance.

Though she wouldn't have expected it, Seth had managed to charm even Jason, quite a feat, since her father had disliked Richard from the start.

The two of them talked about fishing, cars, even politics. After one of their trips to Jackson for dinner, her father had let her know in a subtle way that he thought Seth was a good man.

She didn't have the kind of relationship with her father where she could spill all her own angst to him—all the reasons she knew Seth was bad for her—so after a stunned moment, she had just thanked him for watching Morgan and Cole for her and gone to bed.

No, she couldn't expect any aid from that quarter.

"All right," she said now. "Thanks. I just need to grab my coat."

It wouldn't be so bad, she decided. If she could find a quiet moment while Morgan and Cole were distracted, perhaps on this snowy, moonlit walk, she might be able somehow to find the opportunity—and the strength—to talk to Seth.

Fifteen minutes later, bundled against the cold wind blowing down off the mountains, they walked out into the night, Lucy in the lead, scampering a short way ahead of them.

People in Pine Gulch took their holiday lighting seriously, she had learned the last few weeks. Nearly every house had some kind of holiday decoration, from a string of basic colored lights framing a window to more elaborate displays of reindeer and Santas and full-size nativities.

All the holiday spirit gave the little town a quiet, magical air on a winter evening. They seemed to be the only ones outside and their boots left tracks in the skiff of new snow covering the quiet streets as they walked toward the small downtown.

Seth walked at Morgan's side, easily matching his long-legged stride to her much shorter one, while Jenny walked beside Cole, grateful her son had come along.

The town had its own light display at the small park next to her elementary school and that was their ultimate destination.

Here, the trees were lit with what seemed like millions of tiny multicolored twinkling lights. They were lovely, Jenny thought, though the rest of the display looked as if had been added to piece by piece over the years. A trio of illuminated carolers stood next to a plastic snowman of a different style and size and across the sidewalk from a couple of giant nut-crackers.

Lucy's leash suddenly slipped out of Morgan's hand and the puppy took advantage of the unexpected freedom to race across the park toward the play equipment, her leash dragging through the snow.

"Oh, no!" Morgan exclaimed.

"Don't just stand there like an idiot," Cole snapped. "Go get her."

Seth didn't even say anything, he just raised an eyebrow at the teen. That always seemed to be enough to remind Cole to stow the attitude. This time was no different. After a second, Cole huffed out a breath and went after his sister and the recalcitrant puppy.

As soon as they were out of earshot, Jenny was painfully aware this was the private moment she'd been seeking. She was trying to figure out the right words when Seth spoke.

"What's wrong?" he asked.

She opened her mouth to tell him the truth but the words seemed to catch in her throat. "What makes you think something's wrong?" she stalled.

"You haven't said more than a few words at a time all night. Is something on your mind?"

It was exactly the kind of opening she needed and she knew couldn't put this off anymore, no matter how hard it was. She might not have a better opportunity all night. A careful glance at her children told her they had caught the puppy and were busy watching her scamper through snowdrifts as tall as she was.

Between the three of them, they were making enough racket that anything she might say to Seth wouldn't be overheard.

She released a puff of condensation on a heavy breath. "Yes, actually. Something is on my mind. Seth, I…we can't do this again."

In the colored glow from the lights, she thought she saw some strange emotion leap into his eyes, almost like panic, but it was gone so quickly she thought she must have been mistaken.

"Yeah, you're right," he said after a moment. "We can see the Christmas lights better this way, up close and personal, but it's just too darn cold. Next time we'll take a car so we can cover more ground."

"You know that's not what I mean." She sighed. "This has been wonderful. It has. But—"

Her words ended in a shriek as something cold and wet suddenly exploded in her face.

She brushed snow off and scowled at her offspring, who both surveyed her with expressions so innocent they could have belonged to the angels in the town's crèche.

Even Lucy gazed at her, her little head cocked and her eyes soft and limpid as if butter wouldn't melt in her mouth. Morgan and Cole's innocent looks lasted only seconds before they busted out laughing.

"Oh! That was so not funny!" she exclaimed.

"Don't worry, Jen." Seth bent down for a handful of snow. "I've got your back."

He lobbed the snowball—but instead of aiming it toward her kids, the man she knew perfectly well had been a star baseball pitcher miscalculated by a mile and threw it at her instead, where it thudded against the back of her coat.

Of course, this set Morgan and Cole into more hysterics.

She rounded on him, her glare promising retribution. "I think you are missing the intent of that particular phrase."

Any response he might have made was lost by another snowball, this one launched by Cole, that landed exactly in the center of his chest.

"Kid, that was a big mistake," Seth said, though she didn't miss the glee in his eyes.

From then on, it was full-out war. She took cover behind the plastic snowman and had the satisfaction of hitting both Cole and Seth with solid lobs.

With maternal consideration, she took pity on Morgan, but her daughter repaid her kindness with a sneak attack to her flank. While Jenny was busy evading a concerted attack from the males, Morgan must have skulked along the shrubs until she was just behind her mother, where she had an unobstructed shot. She took full advantage of it, then raced back for cover.

After fifteen minutes or so, Seth finally raised the white flag—or in this case a tan flag, one of his gloves.

"Okay. Enough. Enough!" He stood up. "We're all going to freeze out here if we keep this up. I say we call it a draw and head back to your house for hot chocolate."

As if they had all perfectly choreographed it, she, Morgan and Cole each launched snowballs at him simultaneously, hitting him from every direction while Lucy barked with delight and danced around his feet.

Seth looked down at the dripping mess on his coat and shook his head with a rueful grin. "Remind me not to take on the Boyer clan again unless I have better reinforcements than an Australian shepherd pup."

His laughing gaze met Jenny's, the colored lights gleaming in his eyes. She stared at him and suddenly felt as if an entire truckload of snow had just been dumped on her head.

There in the city park on a cold December night, the truth washed over her stronger than an avalanche, and she had to grab the plastic snowman just to keep upright.

This wasn't just a casual attraction, something she could walk away from without any lasting ramifications.

She was in love with him.

She shivered, chilled right down to her bones, and she couldn't seem to catch her breath.

Oh, how could she have let this happen? She knew he wasn't good for her. From the very beginning, she had told herself he would break her heart but these last few weeks had been so wonderful, she had completely ignored all the warning signs and plunged straight ahead anyway.

And now look what a mess she'd created!

She was in love with a completely inappropriate man, a man who had probably never had a serious relationship in his life.

The gaping maw of heartache beckoned her. She could see it as clearly as if it were in front of her outlined in bright, blinking Christmas lights. Of what use was it to know just what was in store for her, she wondered, since she was suddenly terrified it was far too late to do anything about it?

"I'm cold, Mom. Can we go home?" Morgan's voice jerked her out of her stupor and she somehow managed to catch her breath again.

"Of course, honey. Let's go," she said, forcing a smile that felt like it was made of thin, crackly ice.

They covered the few blocks toward her father's house quickly as the cold wind cut through their snow-dampened clothes like a chainsaw.

When they reached the house, both kids rushed to their respective rooms to change into dry clothes.

Jason was probably in his den—she could hear the TV going—but he didn't come out to greet her and for the first time in a long time, the silence between her and Seth seemed awkward.

He cast a look at the door, looking suddenly anxious to leave. Why? she wondered nervously. He couldn't suspect her feelings, could he?

She cleared her throat. "Would you like to put on something dry from my father's closet?"

"No. I'll just run the truck's heater full-blast on my way home and I'll be dry soon enough."

"Are you sure?"

"Yeah. I'll be fine."

Again they slipped into that awkward silence. Here was where she should tell him she couldn't see him again, she thought. She opened her mouth but he cut her off so abruptly she almost wondered if it was deliberate.

"Thanks again for dinner. It was really delicious," he said.

"Um, you're welcome. Seth—"

"What are you doing tomorrow?"

She blinked, wondering at his apparent urgency. "I don't know. I have a faculty thing Sunday, but tomorrow I just need to take care of some last-minute shopping for the kids. The last Saturday before Christmas is the biggest shopping day of the year, did you know that? A lot of people think it's the day after Thanksgiving but it's not."

She was babbling, she realized, but she couldn't seem to rein in her unruly tongue. Filling up the space with the inconsequential and mundane only delayed the inevitable, she told herself.

"Shopping is on my agenda, too," Seth said, then smiled suddenly, though she thought it looked a little strained. "You know, I could sure use your help."

"My help?"

"I'm not having much luck this year shopping for my brothers' wives or for Natalie and I'm running out of time. I could use a woman's perspective, you know?"

This from the man who seemed to know far more than most women about what they wanted?

"I was planning to head into Jackson Hole," he went on. "Maybe check out some of the galleries. We ought to save gas and go together. What do you think?"

She didn't think he really wanted to know the grim thoughts running through her mind—that she should run far away from him, that she should make this their last goodbye, that her heart was already bracing itself for the pain.

But, oh, she wanted to say yes. One more time. That was all she craved. A few more hours to spend with him. She would go shopping with him in Jackson and store up one last day of priceless memories and then she would have to break things off.

"All right," she said before she changed her mind.

Again he had an odd reaction. Something like relief flickered in his blue eyes.

"I'll pick you up at nine. Does that work?"

At her nod, he stepped forward for the kind of hurried kiss she'd come to expect from him at the end of the night.

She wanted to curl her hands into his parka and hold him tight for a real kiss, the kind they'd shared that night in the garage, the kind she dreamed about at night. But she knew she couldn't, not in her father's entryway with Jason just down the hall, where her children could come running in at any moment.

"Good night," he said, giving her that slow, sexy smile that curled her toes, then he walked out into the night.

She closed the door behind him and leaned against it. She was weak. Weak and stupid and doomed.

The next morning, Seth climbed back into his pickup after dropping Lucy off with Quinn and Marjorie for a play day with her brother.

Her delight at the prospect of a full day of cavorting with another puppy hadn't quite been enough to prevent her from giving him a reproachful look when he headed for the door without her.

He had withstood her canine wiles, though, not wanting anything—not even his adorable but energetic puppy—to get in the way of what he was hoping would be a perfect day.

Even the weather was cooperating. It was a gorgeous

Teton Valley day, the kind they ought to put on travel brochures. The inch or two of new snow from the night before sparkled in the brilliant sunshine and the sky was a bright, stunning blue.

He drove the few blocks from his mom's house to Jenny's, his stomach jumping with anticipation. He wasn't sure he liked the jittery feeling in his gut. It was just a date, after all. Nothing to get so worked up about.

He had been telling himself that all morning while he fed and watered the horses and hurried through the rest of his chores, but he couldn't seem to escape the conclusion that he had to make everything about their time together unforgettable, so incredible she wouldn't be able to bring herself to end things.

He wasn't an idiot. He knew damn well she'd been about to break things off with him the night before while they'd been walking through the town square.

He had seen it in her expressive green eyes, that moment of resignation and resolve, and he'd known a moment of sheer, blind panic before the kids had unknowingly bailed him out by starting their snowball war.

She had agreed to go with him today, though. The way he saw it, he had one last chance to change her mind.

He had to. He didn't even want to think about the alternative. He didn't understand any of this, he just knew he couldn't bear imagining his world without her and the kids in it.

These last few weeks with her had been incredible. He'd never been so fascinated with a woman before. Obsessed, even. He thought about her all the time and he couldn't wait until the next time he would see her.

If she asked him why, he had to admit he wasn't sure he could put a finger on it. It was a hundred different things—the way she pursed her lips when she was concentrating on something, the tenderness in her eyes when she looked at her kids, the little tremble she tried to hide whenever he happened to touch her, even in the most casual way.

She was smart and funny and beautiful, and she had this quiet strength about her he found soothing and incredibly addictive.

He was also amazed how she seemed to bring out the best in everybody around her—even him. When he was with her, he felt like a better man, somebody kind and good and decent.

He wasn't ready to lose all that. Not yet. Maybe after the holidays, though even the thought of that left him with a cold knot in his chest.

He pushed away his nerves as pulled into her driveway. Today he wouldn't think about goodbyes. The sun was shining, the day was perfect, and he would spend the rest of their time together showing her all the reasons she needed him.

"Please! I just want to go home," Jenny practically wailed ten hours later. The bruise around her eye looked dark and ugly—almost as miserable as the blizzard that swirled around his pickup.

"I'm real sorry, ma'am," the highway patrolman at the roadblock to the canyon between Jackson and Pine Gulch leaned across Seth in the driver's seat to say to Jenny in a patient voice, "but I'm afraid nobody's getting through this canyon right now. Between the storm and that jackknifed big rig, the canyon's going to be closed anywhere from three to four more hours. Maybe longer. This is one heck of a nasty storm, coming out of nowhere like it did. It's shut down this whole region and we're recommending that people who don't have to travel stay put until it lets up."

She let out a little sound that sounded suspiciously like a sob. The frazzled highway patrolman gave Seth a dark look before turning back to Jenny.

"I wish I could give you a better option but right now I'm afraid you folks are going to have to turn around and head back into town and find a place to wait out the storm until we open the canyon again. The Aspen is a pretty nice place."

"No!" Jenny and Seth both said sharply.

The patrolman looked a bit taken aback by their vehemence, but there was a long line of cars behind them at the roadblock trying to get through the canyon and Seth knew the man had other frustrated motorists to deal with.

"There are other restaurants in town. You can try to find a hotel room, too. That might be your best bet."

"Thank you for your help," Seth said grimly. "We'll figure something out."

The man waved them on and Seth rolled up his window and turned his truck around to head back into Jackson Hole.

Jenny stared out the windshield, her features stony, and his hands tightened on the steering wheel.

He had screwed up everything. The way things were going, he would be lucky if she ever talked to him again.

He should have paid more attention to the weather, but he had been working so hard to make sure she had an unforgettable time, he hadn't given the gathering clouds much thought.

If he had just paid a little attention to the warning signs, he would have left two hours ago before the storm that forecasters had said would be just a little skiff decided to hit with a vengeance.

They would have made it through the canyon before the semi jackknifed and they would have been home by now. Maybe Jenny would have been basking in the glow of a wonderful day instead of sitting beside him, her features stiff as if she'd been turned to ice by the storm.

How had things taken such a wrong turn? he wondered. He still couldn't quite figure it out.

For much of the day, everything had gone so well, just as he'd planned. Jackson at Christmas was an exciting, dynamic town, bustling with skiers and shoppers and tourists. He and Jenny had had a great time combing through the trendy little stores and galleries to find last-minute gifts for the rest of the people on their respective lists.

With Jenny's help, he had found the perfect gifts for the important women in his life. He'd already bought his mother and Quinn a gift so he didn't need to worry about them.

For Maggie, he bought a matted and framed photograph of a field of mountain wildflowers in the middle of a rainstorm, their hues rich and dramatic. Caroline's gift was some whimsical handmade wind chimes to go with her collection on the Cold Creek patio, and for Natalie, Jenny had steered him to a set of earrings shaped like horses.

Jenny had already bought most of the gifts for her children and just needed some last-minute things. He helped her pick out a wool sweater for her father that would definitely turn some sweet older lady's head.

For Morgan she bought a whole basket full of books and a pair of earrings just like the set he'd bought for Nat and she finally gave in and bought Cole the snowboard he'd been hinting not so subtly about.

Just as Seth had dreamed, Jenny had glowed through

most of the day. She had laughed more than he ever remembered and she had touched him often, taking his arm while they walked, touching him to make a point, even slipping her hand through his as they stood looking at some of the gallery offerings.

And then Cherry Mendenhall had ruined everything.

No. Though it would be easier to blame the other woman, he knew the responsibility for the disaster of the rest of the day rested squarely on his own shoulders.

If only he had paid attention to the weather and left two hours earlier. If only he had picked a different restaurant for their early dinner. Beyond that, if only he'd walked away a few years ago when Cherry had come over to his table at the Cowboy Bar after a business meeting, all tight jeans and pouty lips.

But he hadn't walked away. In fact, idiot that he was, he had invited trouble to sit right down and have herself a drink.

He hadn't really been looking to start anything that night two years ago, but Cherry had been more than enthusiastic, five feet nine inches of warm, curvy, willing woman.

They'd both been a little tipsy—only he hadn't realized until much later that was more the norm than the exception for her. They'd danced, they'd flirted, and to his everlasting regret now, they'd ended up taking the party back to his hotel room.

He'd thought she just wanted a good time and he'd looked her up a few more times when he was in Jackson, but he quickly discovered he'd badly misjudged her.

Suddenly the fun-loving party girl turned clingy and emotional and started calling him all the time, so much so he finally had to change his cell phone number.

He should have handled things far differently. The

decent thing would have been to sit her down and try to explain that they were obviously after different things. But he'd been right in the middle of building the training arena, up to his ears in details, and hadn't had time for that kind of complication. It had seemed easier just to ignore her and hope she would just go away.

The whole situation with her hadn't been one of his better moments and he was ashamed of himself for it all over again.

When he and Jenny walked into the Aspen for a late lunch and he'd seen Cherry sitting at the bar, he'd just about turned around and walked back out again.

He should have, even at the risk of Jenny thinking he was crazy, but he had figured nearly two years had passed since he'd even spoken to the woman. She couldn't hold a grudge that long, no matter how stupid he'd been over the whole thing. And besides, she probably wouldn't even remember him.

That had been mistake number 421 in this whole thing.

They'd been seated immediately, at a secluded booth near the fireplace with a spectacular view overlooking the ski resort. Everything had been going so well—they ordered and sat talking about their holiday plans and watching the skiers. When he'd stretched a casual arm across the top of the booth, Jenny had cuddled closer and he couldn't remember ever feeling so happy.

And then Cherry had passed their table on the way to the ladies' room.

From there, their whole magical day went straight to hell.

She'd caught sight of him snuggling there with Jenny and instead of making a polite retreat as he might have hoped, she marched right over to their table and started spewing all kinds of ugliness at him. He couldn't remember most of it, but he was pretty sure *rat bastard* had been about the mildest thing she'd called him.

He had done his best to calm her down, aware of the increasing attention they were drawing from others in the restaurant and of Jenny sitting horrified beside him.

When she turned on Jenny, though, calling her his latest stupid bitch, Seth's patience wore out. He stood up, thinking he would lead Cherry somewhere more private where he could try to calm her down and at least apologize to her for the lousy way he'd treated her. But when he reached for her arm, she went berserk and swung at him.

Unfortunately, she missed—and somehow hit Jenny instead.

From there, the whole episode turned into a farce. Cherry had instantly burst into hysterical sobs—and Jenny had been the one to sit her down at their booth, have the waiter bring her coffee and comfort her while Seth had stood there feeling like the world's biggest idiot.

"I just loved him so much!" Cherry had sobbed and Jenny had hugged her.

"I know, honey. I know," she murmured, giving him a censorious look out of her good eye across the table.

It turned out Cherry had only been at the restaurant waiting for her roommate's shift in the kitchen to be over so she could get a ride home. After a few more painfully miserable moments while they both commiserated about men in general and him in particular, the other woman came out, gave Seth another dirty look and led Cherry away, along with any chance he had of convincing Jenny he was more than his reputation.

Neither of them touched their food. He tried to explain but Jenny hadn't been in any kind of mood to listen as he tried to convince her he wasn't the jackass he appeared—though right about now, even *he* wasn't so sure about that.

He'd finally given up, paid their check and walked outside, only to discover that while they'd been preoccupied inside the Aspen, a blizzard had hit with a vengeance rivaling only the proverbial scorned woman.

He sighed now as they reached the outskirts of town, wondering at what point he might have been able to salvage the disaster.

He was all those things Cherry had called him and more and he didn't deserve a woman like Jenny.

He pulled into the snow-covered parking lot of the grocery store. "So what do you want to do? We can find somewhere to wait around for the pass to open in three or four hours or we can take our chances and drive down through Kemmerer and back up through Star Valley."

"How long would that take us?" she asked, still without looking at him.

"In this weather, about six hours."

She looked close to tears but didn't say anything.

"Or, like the trooper suggested, we could try to find a hotel room somewhere for the night and head home in the morning. That's probably our safest alternative."

She looked miserable at the idea of spending even another second in his company. Her eye had swollen almost shut and around all that color, her face was pale and withdrawn.

"All right," she finally said.

"We probably won't have an easy time finding a room," he was compelled to warn her. "Between the holidays and the ski season, Jackson hotels are usually pretty full this time of year. I'll give it my best shot but it might take me a while."

"We have all night, don't we?" she said.

Two hours ago, the prospect of a night with her would have had his imagination overheating with all the sensual possibilities.

Now he thought he'd almost rather walk barefoot over the pass in this blizzard than have to sit by all night and watch her slip further away from him.

Chapter Thirteen

Barely an hour later, Jenny sat ensconced in a plump armchair pulled up to a crackling fire.

"I'm sorry to do this to you, Dad," she said into her cell phone, "but the storm came up out of nowhere. How is it there?"

"We've got a couple inches but it looks like more is on the way. If this keeps up, you're going to think it never stops snowing around here."

"Does it?" she asked.

"Sure. Round about June." Her dad laughed and Jenny wished she had the capacity to find anything amusing right about now. Her sense of humor seemed to have deserted her.

"Seth talked about trying to push our way through as soon as they open the pass again but even under the best-case scenario, we probably wouldn't make it home until two or three in the morning."

"There's no sense in that. Just stay put. We'll be fine. Morgan and I are watching a great kung fu movie and Cole is on the computer instant-messaging his friends back in Seattle. Are you sure you're okay?"

With a sigh, Jenny looked around the beautiful three-room suite with its massive king-size canopy bed, the matching robes hanging on a hook by the bathroom, the soft rug in front of the fireplace.

Trust Seth to come up with the only room left in town—the honeymoon suite of an elegant bed-and-breakfast she had heard touted as one of the ten most romantic small inns in the West.

She couldn't speak for the rest of the place but the honeymoon suite just screamed romance. Everything about it—from the matching armchairs to the huge whirlpool tub—was designed with lovers in mind.

How on earth was she supposed to be able to resist Seth Dalton under these circumstances?

"I'm fine," she finally lied to her father. Black eye notwithstanding, she reminded herself firmly.

If she had trouble remembering why she needed to keep her distance from Seth, she only needed to find a mirror. That vivid, iridescent shiner ought to do the trick.

"Don't let Cole I.M. all night. He should be off by ten. If he gives you any trouble about it, call me and I'll set him straight."

"We'll be fine. You just stay warm."

At that moment, she heard the key turn in the lock and Seth came in carrying the ice bucket. His reflection in the window looked big and male and gorgeous, and she knew without a doubt keeping warm was definitely not going to be the problem.

"Thanks again," she said to her father. "I'll see you in the morning."

"Don't forget your faculty party."

She winced, wondering if she could find enough makeup in all of Pine Gulch to camouflage her black eye to all her teachers.

"That doesn't even start until six tomorrow night so we should have plenty of time to make it back."

She said her goodbyes to her father and hung up as Seth set the ice bucket down on the dresser.

"Everything okay at home?" he asked.

"Fine. Dad's got everything under control. I shouldn't worry."

His smile didn't quite reach his eyes. "But you're a mother and that's what you do."

"I suppose."

He sat down in the armchair next to her and she wondered how the elegant romance of the room only seemed to make him that much more dangerously male.

"You're lucky you've got your father to help you with Cole and Morgan," he said.

"Moving here has worked out well in that regard."

"But not in others?"

If she had stayed in Seattle, she would have been safe. She wouldn't be trapped here in a romantic inn trying to fight her attraction to a man who would dump a woman without even telling her.

"This is a nice room your friend was able to find for us," she said instead. "I guess it helps to know the manager."

She hadn't missed the familiarity between the two when they checked in and she had to wonder if there were any females in the three-state region Seth *didn't* know.

"Yeah, Sierra's great. She grew up in Pine Gulch before she moved to the big time here in Jackson. We've been friends forever."

More than friends at some point, unless Jenny missed

her guess, but she decided not to press it. She really didn't want to know anyway.

"Are you hungry?" he asked. "You didn't eat much at dinner."

"I'm fine." she said.

He lapsed into silence and she was acutely aware of him and the long evening stretching out ahead of them.

"Oh, I almost forgot. Along with spare toiletries, Sierra gave me a couple of cold packs from the hotel first aid kit for your eye."

He grabbed one from the dresser, popped it to activate the chemicals, then held it out to her.

Their hands brushed as she took it from him and despite everything, her whole body seemed to sigh a welcome at his nearness.

"Thank you," Jenny murmured, grateful for the slap of cold as she held it to her eye. "I'm sure she must have wondered why I look as though I just went ten rounds with a prizefighter."

He lifted a shoulder in a shrug. "I told her the truth. That you stepped in the way of a punch aimed at me. She didn't seem to find that hard to believe at all."

"You mentioned the vengeful ex-lover, I assume."

He winced. "I did. For some reason, she *really* didn't find that part hard to believe."

Despite her best intentions not to let him charm her, a smile slipped out at his rueful tone.

Regret clouded the pure blue of his eyes as he looked at her holding the ice pack to her eye. "Jenny, I have to tell you again how sorry I am that all this happened. Cherry, the storm, all of it. I wanted today to be perfect for you, but as usual, I've only succeeded in making a mess of everything."

He looked so earnestly miserable that she could feel

a little more of her resolve erode away like the sea nibbling at the sand.

"Why did you want everything to be perfect?" she asked.

He said nothing for several moments, then he sighed. "I didn't want you to break things off with me. That's what you planned to do last night, wasn't it?"

She stared. How had he figured it out? "You are entirely too good at reading women."

"No. Just you."

His words seemed to hang in the air between them. She wanted to protest that he didn't know her at all, but she knew it would be an outright lie. He just might know her better than anybody else ever had, something she found terrifying.

"Why, though? That's what I can't quite figure out," he went on. "Why were you all set to push me away? I could understand if you never wanted to see me again after the disaster of today. Any woman would probably feel the same. But before this, I thought things were going well. You seemed happy. I know I was happy. Did I completely misread things?"

He looked so bewildered she had to fight the urge to reach across the space between them and grab his hand.

Physical contact between them right now was not a good idea. In fact, if she were smart, she would probably lock herself in the bathroom all night until the snow cleared and she could be safely back in Pine Gulch.

How could she tell him that all the reasons she'd been compelled to end things with him had just crystallized into the form of that poor, misguided girl in the restaurant?

Cherry Mendenhall was *Jenny,* with a little more time and few more drinks under her belt. Oh, she wanted to think she would never throw a drunken scene in a restaurant over him but she would *want* to and that seemed just as demoralizing.

When he moved on to his next conquest—as she had absolutely no doubt he would—he would leave her heart scraped raw and she would be as devastated and lost as Cherry.

"They were going well," she finally said.

"So why were you putting on the brakes?"

She couldn't tell him the truth so she avoided the subject. "You can't honestly tell me your heart would have been broken if you didn't see me anymore, Seth."

"Oh, can't I?" he murmured, his eyes an intense blue in the dancing firelight.

She studied him for a long moment, her heart pounding, then reality intruded and she shook her head, forcing a smile. "Your reputation doesn't do you justice. You almost had me believing you."

"Screw my reputation!" He rose and towered over her suddenly, all the easy amiability gone from his posture, reminding her again that a big, dangerous man lurked beneath all the smiles and flirtation.

"Screw my reputation," he repeated. "Just for one second, forget everything you might have heard about me from mean-hearted people who ought to just keep their frigging mouths shut. If today hadn't happened with Cherry and you'd never heard any of the gossip— if you only had to judge me on the man you've come to know this last month—would you still be so damn cynical and judgmental? Or would you at least be open to the possibility that I might care about you?"

Her answer seemed important to him in a way she couldn't understand so she pondered it.

"I don't know," she finally had to admit. "I'm not the best judge of character when it comes to men."

"You don't think you can trust your own instincts, just because your ex was a bastard and messed around on you?"

She flushed. "Who told you that?"

The anger seemed to leave him as suddenly as it appeared and he slid back into the armchair, looking tired somehow.

"Cole. One day when we were working on the car, he told me his dad walked out on you for his twenty-year-old girlfriend. He abandoned all of you to move to Europe with her. Cole calls him Dick the Prick, by the way. Sounds pretty apt, from what he's told me."

A startled laugh escaped her. Oh, Richard would hate that. "It's apt. Believe me."

She had never heard Cole say anything derogatory about his father and she couldn't quite fathom him telling Seth all that. From the way Cole had treated her since Richard had moved to France, she had been certain he blamed her for his father's defection. What was it about Seth that made Cole trust him with the truth? Her son had opened up to this man in a way he hadn't to the family therapist they'd seen after the divorce, or to her, or to his grandfather.

She didn't understand it, but she could only be grateful for the comfort it gave her to know that perhaps her son didn't hate her after all.

"Until the day Richard told me he was leaving, I had no idea he was cheating on me. I was completely oblivious. I thought I had the perfect life, the perfect marriage. You wouldn't believe how smug and self-righteous I was. I even used to give relationship advice to my friends! And all the time, my husband was sleeping with another woman."

"You think that automatically makes you a lousy

judge of character? Because you made one mistake? Because you didn't know your husband was cheating? Maybe he was just a master manipulator."

She definitely could see that now, but at the time she'd been completely oblivious to it. What if Seth was doing the same thing to her and she was too blind to see it?

"Maybe you are, too. How do I know you're not cut from the same cloth, that you won't say anything, do anything, to charm your way into a woman's bed?"

She regretted her words as soon as she said them, especially when his eyes darkened with some emotion that looked suspiciously like hurt. "Is that really what you think?"

"I don't want to think that," she whispered. "When I'm with you, I want to believe every word you tell me. It's when I step back that all the doubts crowd in and I can't understand what we're doing here. Why would a man like you even want to be with me?"

His laugh sounded raspy and rough. "You have no idea what you do to me, do you?"

She blinked, then her heart seemed to flutter when he stood up and pulled her to her feet as well.

"Fine," he growled. "I'll show you."

He kissed her and the heat in it scorched her right to her bare toes. She curled them into the carpet and just held on, swept into the firestorm he stirred inside her.

After those first fiery moments that left her nerve endings ablaze, he gentled the kiss and his mouth was achingly tender.

"I want you, Jenny," he said softly against her mouth, sending tiny ripples of need through her. "But if this was only about sex, I could have done something about it weeks ago."

Though she felt boneless and weak from his kiss,

somehow she marshaled enough strength to give him a skeptical look. "You're so sure about that?"

In answer, he kissed her again, until her hands wrapped around his neck and she had to hold on tight to keep from melting onto the carpet.

"Pretty sure, yeah," he murmured, with a supreme confidence she couldn't deny, given the evidence she had just provided him.

"You tremble every time I touch you. Did you know that? Even if I just happen to brush up against you when we're walking somewhere. That's an incredibly arousing thing for a man, to know he has that kind of effect on a woman."

Her face burned. She thought she had hid her reaction so well. It was the height of humiliation to learn he'd known all along.

But his eyes were anything but gloating. "You have no idea how hard it's been for me to keep my hands off you these last few weeks. If this had just been about getting you into bed, we would have been there a long time ago. But if nothing else, that alone should tell you that you mean more to me than that. I haven't pushed you. I've been patient and low-key and noble, while I've been burning up from the inside out."

"Seth—"

Whatever she wanted to say was lost against his mouth when he kissed her again, this time with a slow and gentle tenderness that made her eyes burn with emotion.

"I care about you, Jenny. Not just you but Morgan and Cole, too. There's something between us. Something I've never known before, something I don't quite know what to do with. You scare the hell out of me and that alone ought to tell you this is different than anything I've ever experienced. I've never been afraid of any woman. Well, not since Agnes Arbuckle, my junior-high English teacher."

She smiled, trying to imagine him sitting in a class-room giving book reports and learning to diagram sentences.

"You scare me, too," she murmured, but she defied her own words by tugging him closer and kissing him.

Despite everything, in his arms she felt safe from the storms outside, from the howling wind of her own un-certainties and the lashing, pounding ice crystals of self-doubt.

They stood for a long time wrapped around each other while the fire sparked and hissed. All those tender, frightening emotions of that night in her garage came rushing back and she was helpless against them.

She wasn't sure how—everything seemed a blur but his mouth and his hands and his strength—but somehow they ended up in the bedroom of their suite.

He lowered her to the mattress of the canopy bed, and she shivered as his big, powerful body pressed her into the thick, fluffy comforter. Next to all his hard muscles, she felt small and feminine and wanted.

He gazed at her in the glow from the firelight, his eyes glittering, then he kissed her again and she surren-dered to the magic.

He trailed kisses down her neck and she moaned, writhing as he unerringly found every one of her most sen-sitive spots—and a few she'd never realized were there.

"You smell so good." His voice was rough and aroused. "There's this meadow up in the high country where we take our cattle. In early summer it explodes with wildflowers. Lupine, columbine, Queen Anne's lace. A hundred different colors. There's nothing I love more than riding a horse across it just after a rainstorm, when everything smells fresh and sweet and gorgeous."

He trailed kisses to the V-neck of her sweater, then up the other side again. "Every time I'm near you, I feel like it's June and I'm standing in the middle of that meadow with the sun warm on my face."

Oh, he was good. Everything inside her seemed to stretch and purr and she finally had to slide her mouth to his, just to stop the unbearably seductive flow of his words.

For long moments, they touched and kissed and explored, until she was breathless, trembling with need.

Finally, when she wasn't sure she could bear any more, Seth rolled onto his back, breathing hard.

"We're going to have to stop here, sweetheart. After a month of foreplay, I'm just about at the limit of my self-control where you're concerned."

She shifted her head on the pillow and studied him, those gorgeous eyes hazy with need, those sculpted, masculine features that made her ache just looking at him.

"Stop it," he ordered darkly.

"What?"

"Looking at me like that. You're not making this easier. Sometimes it's hell trying to do the right thing."

He was right. They should stop teasing each other before they passed the point of no return.

She knew making love would be a mistake right now, that she would have to face a mountain of regrets in the morning.

But this might be her only chance with him. Despite his tender words, she knew she couldn't hang on to him for long. Soon enough, she would return to real life. To parent-teacher conferences and doctor appointments and the responsibilities that sometimes seemed more than she could bear.

But for now they were here alone together, sheltered from the storm in this romantic room.

She wanted to live. For once, she wanted to throw caution into the teeth of that blizzard and grab hold of her dreams.

She smiled and reached to touch his face, her fingers curving along his jaw. "Why don't we just stop trying, then?"

He gazed at her for a long, charged heartbeat and she thought for a moment he would be noble and walk away. Then he made a low, aroused sound and kissed her with a ferocity that took her breath away.

He'd been holding all this back, she realized, stunned to her soul as he nipped and tasted.

The hunger rose inside her and she needed closer contact between them. With fingers that trembled, she worked the buttons of his shirt, until all those hard muscles were bared to her hot gaze and her exploring fingers. She smoothed a hand over his chest and was stunned by the rapid pulse of his heart.

He let her touch and explore him for a long time. Finally, his eyes heavy-lidded, he pushed her back against the pillows and pulled off her sweater in one smooth motion, leaving her only in her bra and slacks.

She had to wonder if some subconscious yearning for just this had compelled her to wear something besides her usual no-nonsense white underclothes. Instead, she had picked a pair of black tap pants and a matching lacy bra. She could only be glad for the instinct when his eyes darkened.

"Well, well," he said, his voice low, rough. "Who would have guessed the elementary school principal likes naughty underwear? I think there are hidden depths to you, Ms. Boyer."

She could feel herself blush and cursed her redhead's skin, especially when so much was exposed.

He didn't seem to mind. "You have the most incredible skin I've ever seen," he murmured, then his mouth dipped to the V of her bra. "Pale and creamy, like fresh, warm milk. Except when you blush, then it makes me think of strawberries. Plump, juicy strawberries melting in my mouth."

"I get sunburned just walking to the mailbox. It's a redhead's curse."

She completely forgot her train of thought—why she could possibly think her complexion woes might be of interest to anyone—when his hands reached the front clasp of her bra and he slid the lingerie away from her body.

Suddenly she wasn't convinced this was such a good idea.

Why hadn't she thought this through a little better? Sexy lingerie could only take her so far in situations like this.

She was thirty-six years old and had given birth to two children, one now a teenager. Her stomach hadn't been flat for fourteen years and right about the time she hit thirty, she'd started needing underwires in her bras.

That blasted self-doubt suddenly came rushing back and she wanted to yank the comforter over her. She couldn't compare very favorably to all the sweet young things he was used to.

She braced herself to meet his gaze, suddenly afraid of what she would see there.

She wasn't prepared for the blazing tenderness in his eyes, for the heat and the hunger that seared her.

For a moment, something stunned, almost overwhelmed, flickered in his eyes and she would have given anything to know what he was thinking. He didn't say anything to assuage her curiosity, just continued to gaze at her until she couldn't bear it anymore.

She pulled him to her and lost herself in the storm.

A long time later, after he had divested them both of the rest of their clothing and they had teased and tasted until they were both trembling with need, he framed her face in his hands and kissed her with more of that aching tenderness.

She wrapped her arms around him and held on, their gazes locked, as he entered her. Her entire body seemed to sigh a welcome and she arched to meet him.

"You scare the hell out of me," he repeated softly.

"What?" she teased on a moan, feeling more powerful than she ever had in her life. "A big strong man like you afraid of a little thing like me?"

He repaid her by thrusting deeper until she felt every muscle inside her contract. With one more arch of his body, she climaxed suddenly and wildly, gasping his name as wave after wave of sensation poured over her.

His mouth found hers and his kiss was fierce and possessive as he swallowed the rest of her cries. He gave her only seconds to recover before he thrust into her again. To her astonishment, her body rose instantly to meet him again.

His breathing was ragged as he reached between their bodies and touched her. She exploded again in a hot fireburst of sparks and this time he followed her, his mouth hard on hers as he found release.

He awoke in the night to find himself in a strange bed with a warm woman in his arms and the smell of rain-washed wildflowers surrounding him.

Jenny.

They were snuggled together like spoons, her sweet little derriere pressed against him and his arm resting across a very convenient portion of her anatomy.

He shifted on the pillow so he could see her, that wispy red-gold hair, the delicate line of her jaw, her creamy skin that tasted every bit as delicious as it looked.

A strange tenderness welled up in his chest like the hot springs in the high country above the Cold Creek.

He wasn't used to this complete sense of rightness he experienced with her in his arms.

It was odd for him. He'd always been a little uncomfortable spending the entire night with a woman and was usually pretty good at finding excuses to go home before this particular stage in the game.

But he couldn't imagine a single place on earth he would rather be at this moment than right here with the snow still drifting down outside and Jenny warm and soft in his arms.

She was still asleep. He could feel her breasts rise and fall in an even rhythm against his arm, and he tightened his hold, astonished at the contentment pouring through him.

Was this what his brothers woke to every morning? If so, he wondered how the hell either of them managed to climb out of bed at all.

He'd been with his share of women. More than his share, probably, if truth be told. Right now, he saw all those other encounters for what they were. A desperate, pathetic search for exactly this kind of tenderness, for the close connection he and Jenny had shared.

Everything that had come before seemed suddenly tawdry and cheap and he was ashamed of himself for thinking those quick encounters could ever make him happy.

They might have offered momentary pleasure—he couldn't deny that—but it was like the tiny glow from a birthday candle compared to the million-watt floodlights of joy burning in him with Jenny in his arms.

He didn't have a name for all the emotions pouring through him. He suspected what they might be, but he wasn't sure he was quite ready to admit to them yet.

His arms tightened around her again, and at the movement, she stirred.

"Sorry," he murmured in her ear. "I didn't mean to wake you."

"Is everything okay?" she asked, her voice rough from sleep.

He kissed the long, slender column of her neck and felt that slow, astonishing tremble.

"Oh, much better than okay. Everything is perfect."

Chapter Fourteen

Jenny wasn't sure how many times they made love in the night. She couldn't seem to get enough of this wild heat between them.

This was probably number four. Or maybe five. She wasn't sure, she just knew she had awakened some time before to find sunlight streaming through the window and Seth beside her, his face shadowed with stubble and a certain warmth in his eyes she'd come to know well in the night.

"Looks like the storm's stopped," he said.

They would have to leave soon, she knew, but for now the man she loved with a fierceness that shocked her was here in her arms, and she wasn't ready to let him go.

She kissed him, her hands tracing the hard planes of chest then heading south. She was enjoying the anticipation curling through her—the way his stomach muscles contracted as she touched him—when suddenly her cell phone went off.

During a bored moment a few weeks ago, Morgan had programmed it to play a vocal version of Jingle Bells for the ringtone and they both stared at it as the merry little tune chirped through the room.

"I should get that," she finally said when the singers had sung the first verse and started jingling all the way.

"Do you have to?" He kissed the spot just below her ear he had somehow discovered drove her crazy and she groaned.

She had a wild urge to abandon good sense and let the thing ring, but already that world she feared so much was intruding on their haven. She was a woman with responsibilities and she couldn't just throw them out the window—no matter how much she might want to.

With a deep, regretful sigh, she reached for her phone on the bedside table. "It might be Dad or one of the kids. I have to see."

He sighed and slid away slightly, though he stayed far too close for her to keep a coherent thought.

She didn't recognize the incoming number but she answered it anyway, hoping the caller couldn't hear that ragged edge to her voice.

"Hello?"

There was a pause for three or four seconds. "Jen? Is that you?" she finally heard and her heart sank as she recognized Marcy Weller's voice.

She sat up, pulling the sheets around her.

"Hi Marcy. How are you?"

Her assistant gave a crazed-sounding laugh. "Oh, just dandy. I'm only in charge of planning a dinner party for fifty people in ten hours and the caterer has to pick today of all days to go flaky on me."

The faculty party. She hadn't given it a thought since the day before. How much power did Seth hold over her if he could make her completely forget something she'd been obsessing about for weeks?

In an effort to shore up the sagging morale at the school and to try yet again to make a connection with her staff—some of whom were still resentful the school board had brought in an outsider—she'd decided to dig into her own savings to throw a party for the faculty and staff at the school. Marcy had offered her parents' large, elegant house as the venue since they were traveling during the holidays.

Her vivacious assistant had taken over the party planning, handling all the details and leaving Jenny only to worry.

Which she'd forgotten to do for the last twenty-four hours.

She gathered her thoughts and tried to sound professional and composed. "What do you mean? What's wrong with Allen?"

"Not him. His stupid wife," Marcy exclaimed. "Candy went into labor three weeks early, can you believe it? How can she do this to us? Where are we supposed to come up with a caterer at the last minute?"

Jenny gave a startled laugh, but Marcy went on before she could comment.

"This is just like Candy," Marcy said darkly. "She always hated me. She hasn't changed a bit since she was head cheerleader at high school—she can't stand not being the center of attention."

"I really doubt she planned going into labor just to inconvenience you and ruin our faculty party."

"You don't know her like I do. I wouldn't put anything past her."

Jenny didn't know her at all, she just knew Allen was a great caterer she'd already used twice since she came to Pine Gulch.

"What are we going to do?" Marcy wailed. "Oh, this is a nightmare! Between yesterday's blizzard and now Candy's selfishness, this party is going to be a total bomb."

"Calm down. We'll figure something out. I can't imagine Allen didn't have at least some of the prep work done for the party, since it's only in a few hours."

Marcy drew a breath and Jenny could picture her moving into one of the calming yoga moves from the class she took from Marjorie Dalton that she practiced in times of stress. When she spoke, some of the hysteria seemed to be gone from her voice.

"He tried to tell me everything that was ready for the party but I could hear Candy yelling at him to hurry up in the background and he was so flustered I couldn't make sense of half of it. He did tell me where the spare key is to his kitchen, though."

Jenny rose and started pacing the room, lost in administrative problem-solver mode.

"Okay. Here's what we're going to do. You've got the key and the menu we agreed on. You can run over to Allen's place right now and see if you can figure out how much prep he's finished and how much we still have left to do."

"I can do that. It's only a few blocks away. Better yet, why don't you meet me there? We could do this faster with two of us."

She turned around and saw Seth lounging against the pillows watching her with that light in his eyes again. She abruptly realized she'd left the sheets behind on the bed and was pacing the room dressed in nothing but her cell phone.

She cleared her throat, knowing she would look more foolish if she scrambled back under the blanket, as she wanted to do. Instead she reached for the closest article of clothing—his shirt—and slipped into it.

"Well, there's a bit of a hitch there. I was, um, stranded in Jackson last night by the storm."

"You're in Jackson?" All the panic—and more—returned to Marcy's voice and she spoke the last word about three octaves higher and several decibels louder than the first two. "When I called your house and your dad said to call you on your cell, he didn't say anything about you being out of town!"

"I'm out of town for now," Jenny said, hurrying to calm her. "But I'm sure the roads are clear now and I'll be heading back to Pine Gulch as soon as I can, I promise. I can be back in…"

She gave Seth a questioning look and almost dropped the phone at the expression in his eyes, something murky and unreadable that sent her stomach twirling and had her pulling his shirt more tightly around her.

Those gorgeous shoulders rippled as he shrugged and held up three fingers.

"Three hours," she told Marcy. "Though I'll do everything I can to make it in two and a half."

"That's still not enough time for us to get everything ready!"

"It will all be okay, I promise. Try to call Allen at the hospital to figure out where things stand and see if he can walk us through whatever recipes are left."

Marcy was only slightly mollified to have a plan of action. "Ten hours, Jen. That's all we've got."

"I know. We'll figure it out, I promise."

"We'd better. You know how important this is."

She thought of her faculty and how hard she had worked to earn their trust and acceptance. A good school administrator could accomplish nothing without the support of her teachers and she still had a long way to go for that. She hoped this party might melt some of their reserve.

"I know."

"I hope so. This is my one big chance with Lance and I can't afford to blow it!"

Okay, perhaps she and Marcy weren't quite on the same page here, she thought with a smile. She was desperate to build a team with her faculty while Marcy's motives had more to do with a certain physical education teacher she was interested in.

"You know how long it took me to work up the nerve to ask him to be my date tonight," Marcy went on. "I wanted so much to impress him by throwing this really terrific party and now it's all going to be ruined because of stupid Candy Grumley."

"We'll get through this, I swear. Lance won't know what hit him, okay? Just call me on my cell when you've had a chance to assess the situation in Allen's kitchen."

"I don't want to call you when you're driving, especially in these conditions. I'm sure the roads will still be slick."

She didn't want to tell Marcy not to worry about that since someone else would be at the wheel—especially when that someone was a presently naked and extremely gorgeous Seth Dalton.

She felt herself blush. "Don't worry about that. Just call me."

She wrapped up the call a few moments later and closed her phone to face Seth, who was still watching her with that lazy smile.

She wanted desperately to climb back into that bed with him but she knew it was impossible.

"I've got to get back. I'm...I'm sorry but it's an emergency."

"Sounded urgent."

"That faculty thing I was telling you about. We're having a holiday party tonight. Allen Grumley is catering it for us and his wife has apparently gone into labor three weeks later. Marcy thinks she did it on purpose."

"Candy always was a prima donna."

She picked up a pillow and smacked him with it. "Not you, too! For heaven's sake, can't a woman even go into labor without the world assigning ulterior motives?"

He laughed and fended off her attack, then grabbed her and pulled her to him.

She let out a sigh, regret a heavy ache inside her that she wouldn't share this magic with him again. "I'm sorry, but I really do have to get back to deal with the crisis."

He arched an eyebrow. "In that case, maybe we'd better save time and share the shower."

Sharing a shower turned out not to be the world's most efficient idea after all.

She hadn't really expected it to save any time, but she also hadn't been able to resist one more chance to kiss him and touch him. They made love with slow, almost unbearable tenderness, and she had to hope the shower spray hid her tears.

At last they were on their way. Seth drove his pickup through the snow with his usual competence even under the snowy conditions and she was grateful for his presence.

She spent most of the drive making lists and trying

to figure out what they still needed to accomplish to pull off the party.

An hour or so from Pine Gulch, Marcy called again. "Is this an okay time for you to talk on your cell? The roads aren't too slick?" she asked.

"It's fine," Jenny assured her. "I'm not driving."

In the pause that followed, she could almost hear the wheels in Marcy's head turn as she tried to figure out who Jenny might have gone to Jackson with, but to her relief, her assistant said nothing. She was grateful, since she didn't want to have to lie.

"Okay, things aren't quite the disaster I feared," Marcy said. "The desserts and the appetizers are done and so is the salad. Allen only had about half of the au gratin potatoes ready. Knowing how fast those go around here, I was thinking of having some baked potatoes set out when they're gone."

"Great idea."

"Even I can handle baked potatoes. My mom has two ovens in her kitchen and I can set them on a timer to be finished just as the party's starting. And I can cook the ham at my place, too. He's got those all ready to go."

"Wonderful. It sounds like you've got everything under control."

"Not everything. Here's the sticky part. Remember we were offering ham and Allen's famous coq au vin? He has all the stuff for the chicken but I've got no idea how to throw it together."

Jenny's mind raced. Her skills in the kitchen were not the greatest, though she figured she could follow a recipe if they had one. Coq au vin sounded more than a little challenging. Just the name was enough to make her break out in hives. "Is there something else we could substitute?"

"Any ideas?"

She thought through her poultry repertoire, which was pretty limited to roast chicken and a moderately good recipe for grilled lemon-herb chicken breasts.

"See if you can find a recipe somewhere in Allen's kitchen. I'll be there as soon as I can. Between the two of us, we can probably figure something out. Thanks so much for everything you've done so far. It's a lot of work and I owe you big-time."

"I won't let you down, I promise."

"Just make sure you leave enough time so you can get ready and put on all your sparkly stuff for Lance."

"Are you kidding? I'm not going to all this work to impress him, just to show up in an apron and a pair of jeans!"

Jenny laughed and hung up.

"If we pull this off, it's going to be a miracle," she said after she'd folded her cell phone.

"Anything I can do?" Seth asked. "I'm not a whiz in the kitchen, but I can take orders."

The Pine Gulch gossip mill would just about start spinning off its axis if she showed up at Marcy's house with Seth Dalton in tow as a sous chef.

She mustered a smile. "I think we'll be okay. But thanks."

A muscle tightened in his jaw, but he said nothing for several more miles. Finally when they were nearing the outskirts of town—near where Cole had crashed the GTO—he spoke in a deceptively casual voice.

"Why aren't you taking a date tonight?"

The unexpected question had her pen scratching across the list she had been making.

"How do you know I'm not?"

It was a stupid thing to say, but her only excuse was

that he'd flustered her. Something dark and formidable leaped into his gaze and she swallowed, struck once more by how easy it was to forget his easygoing nature covered a hard, dangerous man.

"Are you?"

"No," she admitted. "I didn't…it didn't seem appropriate."

"Why not?"

"I don't know. I guess because I'm the principal." And because the only man she wanted to take was the last one she ever could.

He was silent for another block or so, then he cast her a long look across the cab of his truck. "Even if you *had* decided to ask a date, you would never in a million years have taken me, would you?"

She did *not* want to have this conversation right now, so close to home and all the things she had to deal with there.

"Seth…" she began, but had no idea where to go after that, so her voice trailed off.

In that single word, Seth heard the hesitation in her voice and knew his suspicion was true. Despite everything, despite these last few wonderful weeks and the incredible night they had just shared, she still was ashamed to be seen with him.

Hurt and anger poured through him in equal measures and his hands tightened on the steering wheel. He wanted to lash out at her, to attack and wound until she bled as he did.

Just then the truck slid on some slush and he had to concentrate to keep control in the slick driving conditions. By the time he did, the hurt had just about overwhelmed the anger.

"I get the picture now," he said quietly. "A guy like me is fine for a little romp in the sack but when it comes to anything deeper, you're not interested."

"That is not true."

"Isn't it?"

"You know things are complicated for me right now."

"Your precious reputation. Right."

She bristled at the scorn in his voice. "I have nothing else *but* my reputation right now, as far as my faculty is concerned. It would be different if I'd been here a year or two and had some kind of track record with them—if they knew me and my capabilities. But right now I'm a wild card and my every move is endlessly dissected and analyzed in the faculty lounge."

"And of course we wouldn't want anybody to suspect you might have a pulse."

"It's more than that! I can't afford for my judgment to be questioned on anything."

"Being seen with me would certainly show lousy judgment on your part. I get it."

It was only a party. Why was he making such a big deal about it? Intellectually, he knew his reaction was out of proportion to the situation. But he couldn't seem to hold back the tide of hurt washing over him.

The whole thing had an oddly familiar feel to it. He tried to figure out why and was almost to her father's house when it hit him like a snowplow coming through the windshield.

It felt familiar because he'd been down this road before. Many times before. He had spent the first twelve years of his life trying to win the approval and acceptance of someone determined to reject him at every turn.

Hank Dalton had been a bastard who'd treated all three of his sons with varying degrees of cruelty.

He had tried—and failed—to mold Wade into a carbon copy of himself. He had disregarded all of Jake's dreams of being a doctor and completely dismissed his middle son's intellect and quest for knowledge. As for Seth, he might as well not have existed for all the notice Hank paid his sickly youngest son.

He remembered how he used to follow his father around, copying his every move—from his cocksure walk to the way he wore his hat to that hard-ass, screw-you stare his father had perfected.

All for nothing. His father hadn't noticed a damn thing except the asthma Seth had no control over.

His jaw tightened. He wasn't that weak, puny kid eager for any scrap a bastard like Hank Dalton might toss at him anymore. Long before the year he turned twelve, when Hank had died, he'd given up on his father ever seeing him as anything other than a worthless runt, always out of breath and clinging to his mother.

He'd come a long way since those days, so far he thought he had put all that behind him. So why did Jennifer Boyer's blunt rejection seem so painfully familiar?

He thought of the night they'd just shared, the heartbreaking intimacy of it and the connection he had never experienced with anyone else. He replayed again the pure, incomparable sweetness of holding her in his arms while she slept and he was astonished and terrified by the raw emotion welling up in his throat.

He swallowed it down, forcing it back by concentrating on the road.

"I see," he said when he trusted his voice again.

She sent him a searching look and he gave a casual shrug, determined not to let her see how she had eviscerated him. "No big deal. I've got plenty of things I could do tonight."

He must not have been completely successful at hiding his hurt because her eyes darkened.

"I'm sorry, Seth. But please try to see this from my perspective."

"Oh, I do," he assured her. "Nothing possibly could be worse than letting the faculty and staff at Pine Gulch Elementary see their new respectable principal hanging out with the town's biggest hellion. What a nightmare that would be for you."

"You don't need to use sarcasm."

"Yeah, I do." The tenuous rope he had on his emotions frayed abruptly. "Dammit, Jen. How can you even care what other people think, after what we've just shared?"

"What did we share? I slept with you, but that certainly doesn't make me unique among the female population of Pine Gulch."

Ah. Direct hit. He almost swayed from the force of it, but drew in a breath to steel himself against the pain. "It was more than that and you know it."

Her hands clenched in her lap and she was trembling as though she was standing out in the snow with bare feet.

"It was a mistake," she said quietly. "A lapse of judgment on my part brought on by the storm and the enforced intimacy of the situation. One that won't happen again. I can't see you anymore, Seth."

He should have expected it, but somehow he hadn't been prepared for the panic burning through him, raw and terrifying. He wanted to rage and yell and beg her not to cut him off from something that suddenly seemed as vital to him as breathing.

There was nothing he could say, though, nothing he could do to fix this and he could only be grateful they had reached her father's house.

He pulled into the driveway and sat there, his hands on the steering wheel.

"That's probably for the best," he finally said, though everything in him howled in protest at the outright lie. "I won't be your guilty secret, Jen. Some kind of stud you turn to when you're bored or lonely. I care about you. Hell, I think I might even be in love with you."

Her gaze flashed to his and he saw shock and disbelief there but he plowed forward.

"I don't know. This is all new to me." His laugh was rough and scored his throat as though he'd swallowed a dozen razor blades. "Can you believe that? The hellion of Pine Gulch has never been in love before."

He didn't give her a chance to respond. "But if that's what this is, I don't want it. At least not with you. I can't love a woman without the guts to take a chance on something that could be wonderful."

"Or miserable," she whispered.

"Or miserable," he agreed. "But we'll never know, will we? Because you've decided I'm not good enough for you."

"That is not true!"

"Isn't it?" He felt a hundred years old, suddenly. Old and tired and terribly, terribly sad.

On bones that seemed to creak and groan, he climbed out and walked around to her side of the truck, opening the door pointedly. "Goodbye, Jen. You've got a whole list of things to do before your big party so I'm sure you'll forgive me if I don't come in."

She didn't move for a long moment, the only color in her face the shiner Cherry had delivered. Finally she slid down, hesitated for just an instant—just long enough for him to pray she would fall into his arms, that she would kiss him and make all of this go away.

But she didn't. She didn't even look at him again. She just seemed to square her shoulders, then she walked away.

He waited just long enough for her to open the front door, then he climbed back into his truck and backed out of the driveway—heading toward the misery he knew was the rest of his life.

Chapter Fifteen

It was tough to get a good drunk on at one in the afternoon. Oh, he tried, but all he had in the house was beer and he didn't feel like driving back into town for something harder.

After two Sam Adams, he decided it was pretty pathetic to sit there in his cold house with only Lucy for company, wasting perfectly good beer when he wasn't at all in the mood.

Driven by emotions he didn't know how to deal with, he finally decided to channel all this restless energy into trying to catch up on the work he'd neglected in order to take Jenny shopping. He grabbed his coat and hat, whistled for Lucy and headed out through the cold to the indoor arena.

It didn't help much, he decided an hour later atop a big, rawboned bay mare he was training for a client. A little but not much.

His chest still ached and he couldn't quite keep the knot out of his throat, but at least he wasn't sitting around feeling sorry for himself.

He was roping one of the iron calf heads they used for training when Lucy suddenly barked a happy greeting. The loop landed yards shy of the mark as he turned quickly in the saddle to see who had come in.

The hope in his chest died a quick and painful death when he saw his oldest brother leaning against the top rail of the arena gate.

He gave a mental groan. This was just what he needed. His brother tended to see far too much and was never shy about doling out advice, wanted or not.

As tempted as he was to ignore Wade and just keep on roping, he knew he would only be delaying the inevitable. He took his time coiling the rope, then nudged the horse toward the fence.

"She's looking good," Wade said when he neared.

He dismounted. "Yeah. I imagine Jimmy Harding will be pleased with her when I'm done."

"For what he's paying you to train her, she ought to be able to stand on her back legs and salute the flag as it goes by."

He bristled. Here was the fight he was itching for. How considerate of Wade to hand deliver it. Though the fence was between them, that didn't stop him from climbing in his brother's face. "Are you implying Harding's not going to get his money's worth?"

Wade sniffed, then raised an eyebrow at the half-empty beer bottle Seth had brought along and left on the railing a few yards away. "Not at all. I just wondered if your usual training method involves working with a horse when you're half plastered."

"I had exactly two and a half beers! What are you, working for the state alcohol commission?"

"Nope. Just a concerned brother."

"Who should learn to mind his own damn business," Seth snarled, yanking the saddle off the horse.

Wade just watched him for a long moment while Seth led the horse back to her stall.

"You want to talk about it?"

"What?" He grabbed a brush and started grooming the horse.

"Whatever has your boxers in a twist."

"Nothing."

"You sure?"

"Fairly, yeah," he drawled. "Contrary to popular belief, I think I know my own mind."

"I never said you didn't. But do you know your own strength? Because if you tug that brush much harder, Jimmy Harding is going to look mighty peculiar riding his bald horse."

He froze when he realized what he was doing. He let out a breath and eased up a little then pulled off the bridle and gave the horse one last pat before he let himself out of her stall to face his brother.

"You want me to talk about what's bothering me? Sure. I'll talk about it. How's this? I've got this brother with a beautiful wife and three great kids, one more on the way. His life is frigging perfect, which makes him annoying as hell to be around, especially since he thinks he knows every damn thing in the universe."

Wade seemed in a particularly jovial mood because even that direct attack didn't seem to get his goat, to Seth's frustration. He only gave a cheerful smile that made Seth want to take out a few teeth. "If I knew everything, I wouldn't need to ask what has you drinking two and a half beers in the middle of the afternoon, would I?"

Seth released a slow breath. None of this was Wade's fault. Venting his hurt and rage at Jenny on his relatively innocent brother was unfair and slightly juvenile.

He was bigger than this. A few years ago he probably couldn't have said the same thing, but he'd come a long way in those few years, thanks in great measure to Wade's astonishing confidence in him.

If not for his brother's encouragement and support, Seth might never have found the courage to follow his dreams and build this horse arena, diverting Cold Creek resources in an effort to diversify and build up the equine operations of the ranch.

His brother had placed a great deal of faith in him the last two years. He deserved better than to be sacrificed to the sharp edge of Seth's temper.

"Don't worry about it," he managed after a minute. "I'm sure I'll be fine in a day or two."

He paused, feeling awkward as a brand-new boot. "Sorry to take my bad mood out on you."

Wade studied him and he had to wonder how much of his turmoil showed up on his features, especially at his brother's next words.

"Does your lousy mood have anything to do with the lovely new elementary school principal you took to Jackson yesterday?"

He could feel a muscle work in his jaw and he fought the urge to pound his fist into that support. With his luck, he would probably not only break his fist but send the whole barn tumbling down around his ears.

"You could say that."

"The great Seth Dalton having woman trouble? This has to be one for the record books."

"Yeah, yeah. Hilarious, isn't it?"

Something in his tone had Wade giving him an even longer look. Whatever his brother saw had him straightening. "Whoa. I was joking about the woman trouble, but this is serious, isn't it? Trouble with a capital L-O-V-E."

Seth made a scornful, snorting kind of noise that didn't convince Wade for a second.

"Carrie said this one was different," his brother said, shaking his head. "She predicted after that day we went up the mountain for Christmas trees that you were going to fall hard, but I couldn't see it. I should have listened to her. That means I owe her dinner at the Spring Creek Ranch. Man, you know how much that place costs?"

He stared at his brother, appalled. "You and your wife bet on my love life?"

Wade grinned, looking worlds different from the surly widower he'd been until Caroline Montgomery blew into their lives. "Yeah, I should know better, shouldn't I? Carrie knows a mark when she sees one. I guess that's what comes from growing up with a con artist for a father."

Quinn Montgomery, Caroline's father and their mother's second husband, had enjoyed a fairly profitable career on the grift until the law had caught up with him a few years before he'd met Marjorie.

Despite his somewhat shady past, all the Dalton sons had come to have a deep affection for the man. How could they help it when he plainly adored their mother and had given her the joyous life she'd been deprived of in her first marriage?

"So what's going on with Jennifer Boyer?" Wade asked. "I'm assuming the shopping trip to Jackson and your unexpected stay didn't go well."

The understatement of the whole damn year.

"Why should I tell you? Remind me again when we became best girlfriends, here?"

"If you can't get advice from your brother with the frigging perfect life, where else can you turn?"

He had a point. Though his brother was only six years older than he was, Wade had been more of a father figure through most of his life than Hank had ever been. The Dalton patriarch had died of a heart attack on Wade's eighteenth birthday and from then on, Wade had stepped up to show Seth by example how a decent man should live his life.

He hadn't always followed his brother's lead but he had always respected him and at least listened to his advice. It couldn't hurt, he decided.

"All right. You want to know what's wrong? I'll tell you. You'll appreciate this, I'm sure. You know how you've spent the last twenty years telling me my wild, reckless ways were going to catch up to me some day? Guess what? Big surprise, you were right."

"Yeah?"

"Did you know my reputation is somewhat tarnished in Pine Gulch?"

"Don't know if I'd say tarnished. Maybe dented a little in spots."

"Well, Jenny Boyer is looking for a saint, apparently. And too bad for me, I lost my halo sometime around my sixteenth birthday."

He waited for some wisecrack from his brother, some "I-told-you-so" kind of gloat but Wade just looked at him, and the sudden compassion in his eyes turned the lump in his throat into a damn boulder. He worked to swallow it, fighting back the horrifying emotion burning his own eyes.

"I'm sorry, man."

"Yeah. It sucks."

"She's wrong about you," Wade said after a moment, looking about as uncomfortable as Seth was with this conversation. "You might not be a saint but beneath all those dents, you're a good man."

"Uh, thanks. I think."

"You are. You're a hard worker, you're about the most honest man I know, you always dance with all the wallflowers at any party, and you're the first one I'd pick to back me up in a fight. I'm proud of you, Seth. I haven't said that nearly enough over the years, but I am."

He placed a hand on Seth's shoulder for just a moment then let it drop, to Seth's vast relief. Much more of this and he'd be bawling like a just-weaned calf.

"Come on down to the house for dinner, why don't you? Caroline's fixed a roast and some of those twice-baked potatoes you like so much. I think Nat might have even made a cake."

He mustered a smile, wondering if he'd always be the bachelor uncle his brothers would have to leave a place for at the table. "Thanks anyway, but I've got some things to do here. I'm not very good company anyway."

"You know the kitchen's always open if you change your mind."

"Right. Thanks."

Wade left and Seth leaned against the stall railing for a long time watching Jimmy Harding's mare munch her feed and wondering how long it took to heal a broken heart.

"Everything is perfect. I can't believe we pulled it off!"

Hundreds of twinkling lights reflected off the tiny sparkles of glitter in Marcy's upswept hair but they didn't hold a candle to the brilliant glow in her eyes.

From somewhere deep inside, Jenny forced a smile for her giddy assistant. "You did all the work and you deserve every bit of the credit."

"Ha. I was a wreck. You're the one who came through with the coq au vin. Everyone's been raving about it and they can't believe you fixed it all by yourself! I don't know how you did it."

Jenny had to admit, she had no idea. She had been so numb after her fight with Seth that she could barely remember anything after he dropped her off and drove away.

I care about you. Hell, I think I might even be in love with you.

As they'd been doing for hours, his words seemed to ricochet through her mind, bouncing off every available surface.

It couldn't be true. He was only saying that because he was like a thwarted child, willing to say anything to get his way.

No. That was unfair and didn't mesh at all with the man she'd come to know these last weeks. He had never lied to her and she couldn't imagine he would start with such a whopper.

Did that mean he had been sincere?

Despite the room full of people she knew she should be working hard to impress with her warmth and wit, she couldn't seem to think about anything else but those stunning words.

"Is everything okay?" Marcy asked, jerking Jenny back to their conversation.

"Sorry. Everything is great. Look what a wonderful time everyone is having and it's all because of you."

It *was* a great party, one she was sure everyone would remember for years. The food had been delicious, the company entertaining and everyone but her seemed to be in a holiday mood.

"I mean it, Marcy, you saved my bacon on this one."

Her assistant looked pleased with the compliment but she continued to look at Jenny with concern.

"Too bad you're not enjoying it," she said.

Jenny started. Was she that transparent? "Of course I am!" she lied. "Why would you say that?"

"You've only been looking at the clock every five minutes and you haven't left the kitchen for long all night. Keep it up and your faculty is going to think you don't want to spend time with them."

"That's not it at all," she exclaimed, horrified she might have given that impression. "I just… It's been a rough day, that's all."

Marcy arched an eyebrow. "Does your rough day have anything to do with the shiner you got from one of Seth Dalton's ex-girlfriends?"

The platter of finger food she'd been replenishing at the buffet table nearly slipped out of her hands and she looked around frantically to be sure no one else overheard.

"You know?" she hissed

Marcy gave her a rueful look. "My cousin Darlene works at the Aspen during the ski season. She makes major cash in tips, let me tell you. One time Harrison Ford came in and left her fifty bucks! She said he's even better-looking in person than on-screen. Anyway, she said she saw you and Seth Dalton having dinner. She knew Seth, of course—who, by the way, she says is better-looking than even Harrison Ford. And she recognized you because she dropped her little brother off one day at school. He's in Mr. Nichols's fifth-grade class."

Marcy snagged a chicken roll from the plate and popped it into her mouth before going on. "So, Amy says you were enjoying your meal when suddenly another waitress's roommate comes over and starts making this big scene about how Seth dumped her. Amy was in the kitchen and didn't see the whole thing but she said this girl tried to slug Seth but hit you instead."

Jenny couldn't seem to breathe and knew her cheeks must be ablaze with horrified color. "Does everyone know?"

Marcy shrugged. "I doubt it. Everyone's been asking me if I knew what happened to your eye and I just told them the same story you told, you know, about slipping on an icy step. I figure it's none of their business."

Before Jenny could thank her for that, at least, one of the third-grade teachers approached them.

Susan Smoot was a widow who had taught at the school for thirty years. Rumor had it the other woman had had her eye on the principal's office for a long time and Jenny knew she had been one of her most vocal critics when the school board opted to go outside the district to hire her.

She was a formidable enemy—though Jenny had a feeling she could be a powerful ally, as well.

"Thank you for the party, Ms. Boyer. Everything was delicious."

Though she was still rocked by Marcy's revelation, Jenny managed to put it away for now and smile. This was the warmest snippet of conversation she'd ever received from the woman and she didn't want to ruin it.

"Thank you, Susan. Please, I've been here for three months now. When do you think you might consider calling me Jennifer?"

The teacher's mouth twitched but Jenny couldn't really tell if it was a smile. "If you do this again next year, you might want to have it someplace where those of us who don't like the loud garbage that passes for music these days can find a place to hear ourselves think."

"Great idea," she said.

Susan's gaze fixed on the black eye that stood out no matter how she tried to camouflage it with makeup. "And you know, the best thing for icy steps is to sprinkle a little kitty litter on it, Jennifer. Works better than salt and won't kill your flowerbeds in the spring."

"I'll keep that in mind. Thank you."

As soon as the other woman left, Jenny turned quickly back to Marcy and dragged her into the kitchen for a little privacy. "Who else do you think knows I was in Jackson with Seth Dalton?" she asked.

Marcy looked taken aback by the frantic note in her voice. "I don't know. Why does it matter?"

"How can you ask that? Of course it matters! Do you think Susan Smoot would find it an amusing little anecdote that I was decked by one of Seth's jealous ex-lovers? Or even that I was in Jackson having dinner with him in the first place?"

Marcy made a scornful noise. "Let me tell you about Sue Smoot. Most of the time her husband, Carl, was a fine, upstanding citizen. President of the Lions Club, first tenor in the church choir, the whole thing. But every once in a while he'd go on a holy tear and get completely loaded. Before he retired, my dad was the police chief and he used to come home with all kinds of stories about that crazy Carl Smoot. One time he took a shotgun and sprayed every single stop sign in town. Every one! Sue stuck by him through it all. I figure she can't throw any stones at you just for having dinner in Jackson with Seth Dalton on the same night some woman decides to go mental."

"I shouldn't have been there with him. It was a mistake."

"Are you kidding? Any woman who finds herself on the receiving end of that man's undivided attention ought to get down on her knees and consider herself blessed."

She stared at her assistant. "He's a player! Everybody says so. He dates a different woman every day."

"Not true. Maybe he used to a few years ago but ever since the Cold Creek started their horse operation, he's been a different man. He still likes a good party, but he's settled down a lot now that he has some focus."

"I heard you talking to Ashley Barnes that day in the office when she was upset he didn't call her back. You told her about the Seth Dalton School of Broncbusting. You said he was a dog!"

"No, *Ashley* said he was a dog. If you remember, I said he was a good guy, just a little on the rowdy side. He is. His blood might run a bit hot, but that's not such a bad thing, if you ask me, as long as he finds the right woman to help him channel it."

"I'm not that woman!"

Marcy smiled, the sparkles in her hair reflecting the recessed lights in the kitchen. "I don't know. Darlene said he looked whipped in the restaurant before the big scene with the other girl. She said the two of you were holding hands and everything."

I care about you. Hell, I think I might even be in love with you.

She shivered but before she could say anything, Lance Tyler poked his head inside the kitchen. "Marcy, why are you hiding out in here? Are you going to make me dance with Mrs. Christopher all night?"

"Sorry. I'm coming."

She gave Jenny a quick hug and took one last parting shot. "You know," she whispered in her ear so the P.E. teacher couldn't hear, "somewhere out there is a rider

who can tame even the wildest bronc. You'll never know
if you don't climb on."

After she left, Jenny leaned against the counter, her
mind whirling.

*I can't love a woman without the guts to take a
chance on something that could be wonderful.*

His words echoed in her ears, louder than the music
from the other room, louder than the dishwasher busily
churning away beside her.

The ache in her chest seemed unbearable and she
pressed a hand to it, then felt something crack away
under her fingers, something hard and brittle.

She was a fool. A scared, stupid fool.

She loved him. With all her heart she loved him, and
she was throwing away any chance they might have
together because she was too afraid to trust him—and
more afraid to trust herself and her own instincts.

She was so worried about what other people thought
that she refused to pay attention to those instincts. She
didn't deserve the respect she was so desperate to earn
from her faculty, not if she couldn't make up her own
mind about what was good and right and couldn't stand
up for those decisions, even if she faced criticism for them.

Seth was a good man. A kind, decent, *wonderful*
man, who had done nothing but open his life and his
heart to her and her family.

Sweet assurance flowed through her and she remembered the tenderness in his eyes the night before, how
safe and warm and cherished he made her feel.

She straightened from the counter. She had to find
him, right this moment, to see if she had completely
ruined everything or if there might be any chance they
could salvage something from the wreckage she had left
behind with her stupidity.

She rushed out of the kitchen and blinked, a little disoriented to find the lights and the music and the people. The party was still going strong—her party, the one she had thought so vitally important.

How could she leave in the middle of it?

No, she was going to trust her instincts on this one. She had to find Seth now, tonight, before she lost her nerve.

Marcy and Lance danced by at that moment and she stepped forward and grabbed her before she could whirl away again.

"Marcy, I have to go. I…I'm sorry. I'll explain later."

Her friend gave her a careful look, then grinned with delight. "I don't think you need to explain."

She smiled back, the first genuine one she'd felt since she walked away from Seth.

"You were right. I want my eight seconds. No. More than that. I want forever."

Chapter Sixteen

Seth stood just inside the doorway to the Bandito, wondering what the hell he was doing there.

For some crazy reason, he thought his favorite haunt would be just the thing to lift him out of his misery. Usually he loved walking inside the honky tonk—the clink of pool cues setting shots, the music, loud and raucous, the smell of barley and hops and people having a good time. Most of all, he loved the chorus of greetings he received every time he walked in.

This had always been his place, the one spot where he wasn't just Wade and Jake Dalton's wild and reckless kid brother.

But now as he looked at the string of blinking Christmas lights strung across the mirror behind the bar, the cheap foil garlands hanging from the tables and the same faces he'd been seeing here since he was old enough to drink, all he felt was the bitter sting of his own loneliness.

This wasn't what he wanted.

What do you want? he asked himself, but he knew the answer before the question even entered his mind.

Jenny.

He wanted Jenny Boyer, in his arms, in his heart, in his life.

He pushed that dead horse off him and was just about to walk back out into the cold when a buxom blonde wearing a skimpy Mrs. Santa Claus outfit approached him.

"Hey, Seth!" Twice divorced, Dawna McHenry was ten years his senior—and she'd been hitting on him since he turned sixteen. "Haven't seen you around in a while."

"Hey Dawna. It's been a busy few weeks."

"Well, you're here now. That's the important thing. What do you say to a dance?"

One of Alan Jackson's rollicking holiday songs was playing on the jukebox, but Seth couldn't manage to summon even the tiniest spark of enthusiasm to rip up the wooden dance floor right now.

"Sweetheart, you know how much I hate to disappoint a lady. It's nothing personal, I swear, but I'm not much in the mood for dancing tonight. Can I take a rain check, though?"

"You know my umbrella's always open for you, darlin'," she purred, but her smile had slipped a little.

Maybe his own miserable mood opened his eyes a little, but for the first time he saw through her bright cheer to the emptiness beneath. She was just looking for somebody to take away the pain for a while and he was sorry it could never be him.

He wanted to make it better for her, but he didn't

know how until his gaze landed on the middle-aged man sitting at the bar. Roy Gentry was another of the Bandito regulars. A shy cowboy with a small plot of land and his own herd, he never said much to anybody—and became even more tongue-tied when Dawna was near.

"You know who I bet could use a little of that cheering up you're so good at? Roy over there."

Dawna cast a look at the bar. "You think?"

"Oh, yeah," Seth answered. "I bet he gets real lonely all by himself in that big house his folks left him, especially this time of year. Why don't you go see if he wants to dance?"

Dawna looked again and he hoped this time she saw beyond Roy's shy awkwardness to the man who never had a mean word to say about anybody and who always put a little extra in the bartender's tip jar.

She gave the cowboy another considering look. "I wouldn't want anybody feelin' bad this time of year. You know, I might just do that."

She flitted away from him and headed toward the bar. Seth lingered long enough to watch her lean in and say something with one of her bright smiles. He couldn't hear over the music but he saw Roy give a quick, forceful shake of his head, then Dawna tugged him off his bar stool anyway and dragged him over to the dance floor.

He wanted to think it was divine providence—or at least a gift from the King—but right at that moment, Elvis starting singing "Blue Christmas" on the juke box. Dawna threw her arms around the cowboy for a slow dance, and poor Roy looked like he didn't know what hit him.

If he'd had a beer right then, he would have lifted it in a salute to the man. *I'm right there with you, brother,* he thought, hoping he and Elvis might have just planted the seeds of something.

Good deed accomplished, he turned to go when he heard a woman's voice calling his name in a question.

For about half a second, he thought about pretending he didn't hear whoever she was and just continuing on his way. But she called his name again and he turned slowly with a sigh.

The ready excuse on his lips slipped away when he saw the tall brunette in slacks and a holiday sweater beaming at him.

"It is you! Hi, Seth. Remember me?"

"My word. Of course I do. Little Amy Roundy." He hugged her, stunned that this pretty, self-assured woman was the same girl he'd known since kindergarten.

"It's Amy Underwood now."

"That's right. Where is the lucky man?"

She made a face. "Pool table. I imagine my brothers are trying to hustle him out of our traveler's checks by now. They have no idea what they're up against. George plays the part of a mild-mannered, polite, slightly clumsy Brit but he'll rip them apart."

He smiled and knew he couldn't leave now, much as he might want to. Amy had been one of his best friends in elementary school and he hadn't seen her in years.

By tacit agreement he steered them both to the only empty booth, where he took the seat across from her. "I hadn't heard you'd crossed to this side of the pond and finally come back for a visit," he said when they were seated. "How's life in the British Isles?"

"Just ducky, love." She smiled and dropped the accent. "Seriously, I love it. I miss my family and the mountains sometimes, but George and I have made a home there."

"What about kids?"

"Three girls. I've got pictures and everything."

She pulled out her cell phone, punched a few buttons, then held it out to him. He spent a minute admiring the image on the screen of three gorgeous little girls with blond curls and their mother's smile.

"What about you? Is there a Mrs. Dalton?"

He summoned a smile from somewhere deep inside. "Two of them. Both married to my brothers."

"You haven't made the big leap?"

He started to make some flippant remark but Amy's stern look caught it before it could escape. He suddenly remembered he could never hide anything from her. She and Maggie Cruz, Jake's wife, had been his best friends in grade school. They were the only kids in his class who hadn't bullied the wheezy runt he'd been.

Hank had just about popped a vein when he found out his youngest son's two best friends were girls but that had only made Seth more determined to keep them.

"No. Not yet," he managed.

Marriage. Now there was something he hadn't given much thought to. His parents' marriage had been a nightmare, enough to sour anybody on the institution. But his brothers had managed to move on and build amazingly happy lives.

For the first time, he started to wonder if he could ever do the same. He thought again of how he'd felt waking up with Jenny in his arms that morning and he suddenly wanted that every day, with a fierce and terrible ache.

Only too bad for him, the woman in question wanted nothing to do with him anymore.

He shifted his attention back to Amy, wondering what she saw in his face to put that soft, sympathetic look in her eyes.

She touched his hand. "You would make a wonderful husband, Seth."

He forced a laugh at that outright hyperbole. "Right. I'm willing to bet if you took a poll of all the women in this room, you would probably be the only one with that opinion."

She looked at him for a long moment then shook her head. "It doesn't matter what they think. If you find the right woman, her opinion is the only important one."

Didn't he just know it?

He must have made some sound because Amy sent him another sympathetic look. "Want to talk about it?"

No. He wanted to hop in the GTO and drive as far and as fast as he could to outrun this pain, this hollow fear that he would be spending the rest of his life alone.

No, he didn't want to talk about it. But something about his old friend's compassion made him want to confide in her.

"How long do you think it will take your Brit to clean up over there at the pool table?"

Jenny drove through the streets of Pine Gulch, a strange mix of anticipation and anxiety churning through her. Would he even be willing to see her when she reached the Cold Creek after the hideous way she had treated him?

She had to try. Even if he slammed the door in her face, at least she would not have to live the rest of her life with regrets, knowing she might have touched the stars.

On the outskirts of town, she drove past the bright lights of the town's single tavern. The Bandito was doing a brisk business tonight, she thought, then took a closer look and nearly drove off the road.

She knew that red car in the parking lot. Seth's brawny GTO hulked in the corner, shiny and sleek and so distinctive she couldn't possibly mistake it for anyone else's car.

So much for sitting at home pining over her.

He was inside the tavern probably having a wonderful time while she was out here dying inside.

She pulled her SUV into an empty space in the parking lot, trying to figure out what she should do. She had two choices. She could go back to the faculty party and get on with the business of forgetting about him, as he had obviously decided to do about her.

Or she could grab hold of the rigging and climb on.

She owed him an apology. By putting so much stock in gossip and rumor about him, she had treated him with terrible unfairness and she had to let him know she was sorry for it.

Even if he decided not to accept her apology, she would at least know she'd tried to offer it.

She turned off her vehicle and slid out, suddenly aware as she stepped onto packed snow of her holiday cocktail dress and high heels. She was going to look conspicuous, foolish, walking into the honky tonk like this.

People would wonder what she was doing there—and when the people in the packed tavern saw her with Seth, rumors would start flying before she would even have time to sit down.

She almost climbed back into her car, then she shook her head. No. She was strong enough to face a few rumors. She wasn't ashamed of her feelings for Seth. She loved him and she wouldn't hide it. Let the whole town see, she thought.

That defiant energy carried her to the front door of the Bandito and just inside, but there she stopped as the panic and self-doubt started to nip at her like an unruly puppy.

She scanned the crowd, already painfully aware of the stares. She didn't see him at first, then when she found him, that little yip of self-doubt turned into a pack of ravaging wolves.

He was sitting in a booth, cozying up to a brunette Jenny didn't recognize, someone tall and shapely and beautiful. Their heads were close together and the woman was laughing at something he said and Jenny felt like her heart had just been ripped out and thrown on the dance floor for everyone to stomp on.

This was stupid. Humiliating tears welled up in her eyes at her own idiocy and she wanted frantically to get out of there, but she felt frozen in place by this wild storm of emotions.

She was just trying to force herself to move when his gaze suddenly shifted from the woman beside him to the doorway where Jenny stood, exposed and heartsick.

Whatever he was saying to the other woman died as he stared at her.

Everything else in the bar—the laughter, the bright lights, the loud, pulsing music—faded away to nothing as their gazes caught and held.

Jenny couldn't breathe suddenly, stunned by the raw emotion in his eyes, pain and joy and something else she couldn't identify.

Her husband had never looked at her like that, she realized. Not once, in all their years of courtship and marriage, had he ever looked at her like she was his salvation, his entire world.

How could she turn away from this? She loved this man. She loved his strength, she loved his goodness, she loved the sweet and healing laughter he had brought into her life.

And she suddenly wanted everyone to know it.

Her pulse sounded louder than the music blaring from the jukebox as she forced herself to move forward on legs suddenly weak and jittery, until she stood at the edge of their booth.

Once she reached her destination, she didn't know where to start. She might have lost her nerve completely except that Seth hadn't looked away from her, even for a second. They stared at each other for a long moment, until the brunette actually broke the silence.

"Hi. You must be Jennifer."

That had her blinking and she managed to wrench her gaze from Seth to look at the woman, who actually seemed very nice, with warm brown eyes and an approachable smile. Too bad Jenny might just have to take a page from Cherry Mendenhall's book and deck her.

"Seth has just been telling me all about you," the woman went on.

She thought she heard Seth make a groaning kind of sound but she couldn't be sure.

"Has he?" It was all she could manage to say.

The other woman gave a smile Jenny would only have called mischievous if had come from one of her students. "Oh, yes. I'm Amy Underwood, an old friend. Sit down, won't you? Here, you can have my seat. I was just leaving to find my husband."

Husband. Right. Husband was good.

"He's sexy and British and I'm crazy about him," the strange woman added with a laugh. "Just in case you were wondering."

"Amy," Seth said in the chiding voice one reserved for old friends.

She laughed again, getting to her feet. "What did I say?" She didn't wait for an answer, just blew him a kiss. "We're in town until after the day after New Year's. Come and meet George and my girls. I want to know how the story ends."

"Yeah," he muttered. "So do I."

She walked away but Jenny remained standing by the booth, unsure where to go from here.

"What are you doing here, Jen?" he said after a long moment. A note of cool reserve had entered his voice and she winced from it even as she knew she deserved it.

"I was wondering if you would like to dance."

He gazed at her and she saw a host of emotions sift through his eyes. "Here?" he finally asked, looking around the crowded tavern.

"Here. Or at the faculty party. Or wherever you would like."

He gazed at her, stunned by her words, by the offer he knew must have cost her dearly.

Already, he was aware of the curious stares in their direction. Tongues were certainly going to wag with tales of the elementary school principal showing up at the local tavern in party clothes and a black eye and immediately sidling up to his table.

She must have known the gossip would start up before she even walked into the place, yet she had come anyway. She had faced her fears, had all but begged for the very scrutiny she claimed to be so eager to avoid.

For him.

He had never been so humbled.

Joy and sweet relief exploded in him, washing away the hurt and bitterness and angry. She was here, coming to him despite her fears and her uncertainties. He had no choice but to take the precious gift she offered and hold it close to his heart.

He reached for her hand and almost yanked her into his arms right there in the Bandito in front of half the town but he knew that would be pushing things. Instead he uncoiled from the booth, threw some money on the table for his drink, and headed for the door, tugging her along behind him.

"Where are we going?" she asked a little breathlessly.

In answer, he pulled her out of the tavern. The cold December air blew through his jacket and he realized he hadn't given this a whole lot of thought, driven only by the need to be alone with her.

He had to kiss her in the next twenty seconds but he wasn't going to make her stand out in the cold for it, not in her skimpy cocktail dress. Thinking fast, he bundled her into the GTO, then slid into the driver's seat and started the engine.

The heater churned out blessed heat and at last he pulled her into his arms and kissed her as he'd been dreaming of doing since the moment they left the inn in Jackson.

She returned his kiss with a warmth and enthusiasm that took his breath away and they embraced there like a couple of hot-blooded high-school kids at an overlook. Much more of this, and they would be steaming up those windows, he thought.

"I've never made out in a muscle car before," she said after a long, heated moment. "It's kind of sexy."

"That's the whole idea," he managed, then lost his train of thought when she trailed kisses down his jawline to the curve of his neck, then back up.

"Can I just say, for your first time, honey, you're doing *great,*" he drawled.

He felt her laughter against his skin and wanted to taste all of it. He dipped his mouth and caught hers again. Despite their playfulness, there was a poignant sweetness to her kiss, a gentle healing that seemed to wash away all the hurt of the afternoon and evening.

"I'm sorry about today," she murmured after a long

moment, framing his face with her hands. "I'm so sorry I hurt you. It was never about you, Seth. It was me and my own insecurities. I was too afraid to rely on my judgment, to trust that the man I was falling in love with would be willing to catch me on the way down."

He almost couldn't speak, overwhelmed by her words. "What changed?" he finally asked, his voice hoarse.

She was quiet for several moments, the only sound the whirr of the heater and the distant bass throb from the music inside the bar. They would have to leave soon, he thought. They couldn't stay in the Bandito parking lot making out all night, but for now he didn't want to move, more content than he'd ever been in his life.

"Did I tell you about the nightmare I had after Morgan's bad asthma attack, the night my car wouldn't start and you drove us to the clinic to meet Jake?"

He shook his head, shifting so he was leaning into the corner of the seat and her cheek was resting against his chest. He held her close, his hand playing in her incredible hair. It wasn't the most comfortable position but he didn't mind as long as he could hold her.

"I dreamed I couldn't find Morgan," she went on. "She was sick and she needed me and no one would help me look for my child. It was a terrible, helpless feeling. I was just about to hit bottom when someone suddenly appeared out of nowhere and starting shoving away obstacles and pushing people back so I could reach my destination and find my child. I couldn't see his face but I knew even before he turned around who it was."

She touched his face, her eyes soft and a tender smile hovering around that lush mouth. Him? She dreamed of wild and rowdy Seth Dalton coming to her rescue like some kind of hero out of a movie?

"My subconscious has always known what I've been

afraid to admit. I need you in my life. I need your strength and your kindness and your laughter."

He pressed his lips to her fingers, wondering if it was possible for a man to burst with joy.

"I love you, Seth. With everything in my heart I love you and I want everyone in the world to know. I want to run ads in the newspaper and send up hot air balloons and climb to the top of a water tower somewhere so I can graffiti it on the side."

He laughed, completely charmed by this side of her.

"Then you would get arrested for vandalism and I'd have to come pay you conjugal visits—which would be hot and all at first but would probably get old after a while. How about you just settle for whispering it in my ear for the rest of your life?"

Jenny blinked at him. The rest of her life? That certainly sounded…permanent. Was the hellion of Pine Gulch actually proposing?

"I know it's early in the game here," he went on, and she could swear there was a hint of color on his cheekbones in the dim light, "but I just want you to know where I stand. I might just have to put my foot down on this one. I love you and I want everything. The house, the dog, the kids, two cars—three if you count the GTO, which we might have to lock up for a few years until Cole learns to drive a hell of a lot better."

He smiled again and kissed her and all her worries and insecurities seemed to curl up and float away. He loved her. This strong, wonderful man loved her, quiet, boring Jennifer Boyer.

She still didn't quite understand it but she wasn't going to waste any more time doubting it, not when his eyes promised a future of laughter and warmth and joy.

"I love you, Jenny," he repeated. "I want everything."

She smiled and touched his face again, those wild and gorgeous features she loved so dearly.

"You drive a hard bargain, cowboy," she murmured. "But I'll see what I can do."

Epilogue

"Call me crazy, but aren't you supposed to be enjoying yourself?"

Seth swallowed the miserly sip of beer he'd just taken, set his tankard down and aimed a cool look at his older brothers across the table at the Bandito.

"I *am* enjoying myself," he answered Wade. "Who says I'm not enjoying myself?"

If he sounded a trace defensive, he had to hope neither Wade nor Jake noticed. To his chagrin, his brothers didn't miss much. Wade raised an eyebrow at Jake and they both snickered.

"I'd say the evidence speaks for itself," Jake answered, "considering you've been nursing that same beer all night and by my count, that's the third woman you've turned down for a dance in about ten minutes."

It was the fourth, but he wasn't about to point that out.

"I guess I just don't feel like dancing tonight," he

said, wondering why the lights in the tavern seemed so harsh, the music uncomfortably loud. "Since when is that against the law?"

Jake and Wade looked at each other again, then both of them laughed.

"I wouldn't say it's against the law, exactly," Wade said with a particularly annoying smirk. "Just against the natural order of things where you're concerned. This is your last night to solidify your reputation. I can't believe you're not taking advantage of it. You're breaking all those poor girls' hearts."

Friday night at the Bandito was hopping. A live band from Sun Valley rocked the place and the battered dance floor teemed with locals and tourists looking for a good time.

Six months ago, he would have been one of them but it was amazing how a few months could change a man. It had changed this one enough that he suddenly decided he'd had enough of the stuffy tavern, especially when he knew the June night outside would be cool and sweet.

He slid out of the booth and stood up. "I appreciate the thought behind this little party but I think I'm going to head on home now. Thanks for the beer."

His brothers both stared at him like he'd stripped naked and started boot-scootin' across the tabletop.

Jake was the first one to speak. "This is your bachelor party and it's barely nine o'clock! I told Maggie not to expect me to roll in until after closing time."

He waited for some similar comment from Wade but his oldest brother was giving him a careful look. "Your feet feeling a little chill there?"

He raised an eyebrow. "Just because I don't feel much like ripping up the town doesn't mean I've got cold feet about getting married tomorrow."

He'd be lying if he didn't say the whole idea of marriage still scared the heck out of him. But he was crazy-mad for Jenny Boyer—more than he'd ever believed it was possible to love someone—and he couldn't even bear the thought of any kind of future that didn't include her.

The last five months had been as close to paradise as he'd ever imagined and he knew things would only get better.

"I don't have cold feet," he repeated.

Before he could say more, his old friend Dawna McHenry approached their table with a big smile on her face.

"Hey there, Seth!"

"Hey, Dawna." He kissed her cheek, thinking how pretty she looked in her pink flowered sundress. Since Christmas, when she'd started dating Roy Gentry, Dawna seemed different. Her hair wasn't so brassy now and she wore it in a softer style.

"Is Roy with you tonight?" he asked.

"Of course. He's over at the bar," Dawna said. Seth followed her gaze and found the quiet cowboy smiling in a bemused, besotted kind of way in their direction. He smiled back, feeling a definite kinship to the man. If Jenny were here, he'd be looking at her with that same expression in his eyes.

Dawna tucked her hand through his arm. "So tomorrow's your big day. I'd ask you to dance but I saw all those other girls who came over here walk away with big old dejected looks on their face."

"Dawna—"

She shook her head and gave his arm a squeeze. "That's all right with me. I just wanted to tell you how happy I am for you and Ms. Boyer. She's one nice lady."

"Thank you. I'll tell her you said so."

"You do that. Good luck tomorrow." She gave his arm another squeeze then kissed him again and turned back to her quiet cowboy.

"Man, I hardly recognize Dawna McHenry these days. I wonder what's gotten into her lately," Wade said.

"She's in love," Jake said. "It changes a person."

He looked at his brothers and thought how those words certainly applied to the Dalton brothers. Wade wasn't the stressed, workaholic widower he'd been before Caroline Montgomery blew into their lives. Since marrying their neighbor Magdalena Cruz, Jake had learned not to be so serious all the time, to find a little enjoyment in life besides his patients.

Seth had probably changed more than either of them. He wanted far different things out of life than he had before Jenny Boyer and her children captured his heart. Where this would have been his idea of a good time six months ago, now he just wanted to go home and wait out the last few hours until their lives merged.

He smiled at his brothers. "Like I said, I do appreciate the effort you boys took to wrench yourself away from your women for the night but I don't think any of us are really enjoying this. I don't really need a bachelor party. Why don't we call it a night?"

He was a little annoyed to see neither brother was paying attention to him. Their gazes were both fixed on the door.

"Uh-oh," Jake said, his voice sounding oddly strangled. "Here comes trouble."

Seth turned around to see what they were both so fascinated by and just about tripped over his boots. Three women had just walked into the Bandito. Like plenty of other women in the tavern, they looked more than a little wild—heavy makeup, teased hair, tight jeans.

His heart seemed churn right out of his chest, especially when the redhead in the middle caught his gaze. She gave him a long, sultry look and sauntered over to their table, her partners in crime right behind her.

Seth suddenly discovered a pressing need to take a long sip of his neglected beer to soothe his parched throat.

"Well, aren't you three a sight?" Wade drawled and the woman on the right gave a pleased grin.

"Aren't we, though?" Caroline said, looking pleased as a little filly with a new fence post. She leaned forward a little and though Seth couldn't seem to wrench his eyes away from the little redhead who owned his heart, he thought he heard Wade swallow hard.

"We decided we were bored with our little bachelorette party, just us girls," Caroline went on. "We thought this might be the place to find us some rowdy cowboys."

"And you got all dressed up and everything," Jake murmured.

"You can blame Marjorie for that," Maggie said, sliding into the booth next to her husband. "We were just playing around with lipstick shades trying to find a good one for Jenny to wear tomorrow and Marjorie seemed to think it was a real hoot to lay it on thick and heavy. We all got a little out of control and before we knew it, here we were looking like we just stepped out of a bad country music video."

"For a pregnant woman, you're pretty hot," Jake said.

"I do what I can," Maggie purred.

Seth continued to stare at Jenny, falling in love with her all over again. It wasn't because she made one heck of a sexy party girl. It was that light in her eyes that hadn't been there five months ago, the joy and the happiness he saw in her face every time she looked at him.

"Hey, cowboy. Feel like dancing?"

The words were barely out of her mouth before he grabbed her arm and hauled her out onto the dance floor. The band obliged them by starting up a slow song—not that it mattered since he would have held her close no matter what they were playing.

He pulled her against him and suddenly he didn't mind the stuffy air or the loud music. With her here, with her soft and sweet in his arms, everything felt right again.

"Sorry we crashed your bachelor party," Jenny said into his ear, her voice pitched just loud enough to be heard over the music. "I thought we should leave you boys alone tonight but I was overruled. I hate to tell you this, but the women in your family are on the formidable side."

"Yeah, you're going to have a real tough time fitting in, aren't you?" he said drily.

She made a face. "Hey, I got all tarted up to come down here. I deserve points for that, at least."

"You can have all the points you want, sweetheart."

He leaned close and whispered in her ear, the way he knew drove her crazy. "I've got a muscle car parked out front. What do you say we drive up to the lake and make out all night?"

She gave that sexy sigh of hers and he was humbled all over again to know this smart, beautiful woman had somehow chosen him.

"That's a tempting offer, cowboy, but I'm afraid I'd better not. I'm getting married in the morning and I'm not sure I could look Father White in the eye with razor burns and love bites."

He grinned, only a little disappointed. They had the rest of their lives and he intended to fill every day of it showing her how much he loved her. "Despite appearances to the contrary right now, I guess I just might make a respectable woman out of you after all, Jenny Boyer."

"Not too respectable, I hope."

He pulled her closer. "That's a promise."

* * * * *

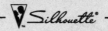

SPECIAL EDITION™

Welcome to Danbury Way— where nothing is as it seems...

Megan Schumacher has managed to maintain a low profile on Danbury Way by keeping the huge success of her graphics business a secret. But when a new client turns out to be a neighbor's sexy ex-husband, rumors of their developing romance quickly start to swirl.

THE RELUCTANT CINDERELLA

by CHRISTINE RIMMER

Available July 2006

Don't miss the first book from the Talk of the Neighborhood miniseries.

HOTEL MARCHAND

Four sisters.
A family legacy.
And someone is out to destroy it.

A captivating new limited continuity, launching June 2006

The most beautiful hotel in New Orleans,
and someone is out to destroy it. But mystery,
danger and some surprising family revelations
and discoveries won't stop the Marchand sisters
from protecting their birthright...
and finding love along the way.

Page-turning drama...

Exotic, glamorous locations...

Intense emotion and passionate seduction...

Sheikhs, princes and billionaire tycoons...

This summer, may we suggest:

THE SHEIKH'S DISOBEDIENT BRIDE

by Jane Porter

On sale June.

AT THE GREEK TYCOON'S BIDDING

by Cathy Williams

On sale July.

THE ITALIAN MILLIONAIRE'S VIRGIN WIFE

On sale August.

With new titles to choose from every month,
discover a world of romance in our books written
by internationally bestselling authors.

HARLEQUIN *Presents*

It's the ultimate in quality romance!

Available wherever Harlequin books are sold.

www.eHarlequin.com

HPGEN06

The Marian priestesses were destroyed long ago,
but their daughters live on. The time has come
for the heiresses to learn of their legacy, to unite
the pieces of a powerful mosaic and bring light to
a secret their ancestors died to protect.

The Madonna Key

Follow their quests each month.

Lost Calling by Evelyn Vaughn,
July 2006

Haunted Echoes by Cindy Dees,
August 2006

Dark Revelations by Lorna Tedder,
September 2006

Shadow Lines by Carol Stephenson,
October 2006

Hidden Sanctuary by Sharron McClellan,
November 2006

Veiled Legacy by Jenna Mills,
December 2006

Seventh Key by Evelyn Vaughn,
January 2007